Adachi and Shimamura

STORY BY **Hitoma Iruma** ART BY **non**

NOVEL **1**

Shimamura
Truant student #1.
A girl with bleached hair and a bit of a ditzy side. She wears more makeup than Adachi does, but sees Adachi as the more beautiful of the two.

Adachi
Truant student #2.
She has a slim figure with few curves. Lately she's struggled with her feelings.

Ping-Pong in Our Uniforms

"Who might this be?"
"This is the Shimamura."
"What's that supposed to mean...?"
"Aha... We meet at last."
"So, uhhh...what's your name?"
"You may call me
 Chikama Yashiro!
 Krrrssshhh...krrrssshhh..."

Fishing for
the Future

"I was wondering, um, if I could sit with you, like, between your legs or something."
"Huh? Sure, I don't mind... What are you doing?"
"Well..."
"My sister does this all the time. It's not weird, right?"
"No, of course not..."

Adachi,
Questioning

"I wanna come over to your house after school today. Is that cool?"

The Isosceles Triangle

"We're doing a duet! ... I actually really appreciate you coming up to sing with me."

"Huh?"

"I'm not great at singing in front of people, you know?"

"Same, actually. I'm glad you're up here with me."

Girls'
Day Out

Table of Contents

1. Ping-Pong in Our Uniforms   11

2. Fishing for the Future   69

3. Adachi, Questioning   113

4. The Isosceles Triangle   157

5. Girls' Day Out   225

Adachi and Shimamura

NOVEL 1

STORY BY
Hitoma Iruma

ILLUSTRATED BY
Non

Seven Seas Entertainment

ADACHI TO SHIMAMURA VOL. 1

© Hitoma Iruma 2013
Edited by Dengeki Bunko
Illustrations by Non

First published in Japan in 2013 by
KADOKAWA CORPORATION, Tokyo.
English translation rights arranged with
KADOKAWA CORPORATION, Tokyo.

Seven Seas press and purchase enquiries can be sent to
Marketing Manager Lianne Sentar at press@gomanga.com.
Information requiring the distribution and purchase of
digital editions is available from Digital Manager CK Russell
at digital@gomanga.com.

Follow Seven Seas Entertainment online at
sevenseasentertainment.com.

TRANSLATION: Molly Lee
COVER DESIGN: Nicky Lim
LOGO DESIGN: George Panella
INTERIOR LAYOUT & DESIGN: Clay Gardner
PROOFREADER: Kat Adler, Stephanie Cohen
LIGHT NOVEL EDITOR: Nibedita Sen
PREPRESS TECHNICIAN: Rhiannon Rasmussen-Silverstein
PRODUCTION MANAGER: Lissa Pattillo
MANAGING EDITOR: Julie Davis
ASSOCIATE PUBLISHER: Adam Arnold
PUBLISHER: Jason DeAngelis

ISBN: 978-1-64505-535-8
Printed in Canada
First Printing: June 2020
10 9 8 7 6 5 4 3 2 1

1. Ping-Pong in Our Uniforms

FROM THE MOMENT Adachi first suggested that we play ping-pong, a hot new fad was born—under the radar, of course, since we were skipping class. The school ping-pong equipment had been left to gather dust on the second floor of the gym, and because we couldn't risk opening the window, the air was stuffy.

Along the edge of the loft overlooking the gym's ground floor ran a green net, a relic from the days when this school had an official ping-pong club. The net's purpose was to ensure that any stray balls remained within the bounds of the second floor. Normally, the two of us sat right against it and whiled away the time chatting in hushed tones. By this point, however, I was getting bored of talking, so I gratefully took Adachi up on the suggestion.

October was almost over, and we'd transitioned to our winter uniforms, though long sleeves were frankly the last thing I wanted to wear in this heat. Fortunately, the warm, sunny weather meant that gym classes were held outside on the athletic field, and *that* meant Adachi and I could have the gym to ourselves. Once we confirmed that we were alone in the building, we got to work setting up the ping-pong table.

"Were you in any clubs in junior high?" Adachi asked as she struggled to affix the net to the table. We'd been skipping class together for about a month or so, but I guess the topic of school clubs had never come up before.

"I was on the basketball team, actually. I was really passionate about it, too. I always stayed late to run drills."

"Huh. I didn't peg you as a basketball player," she mused, probably because I didn't seem all that tall compared to her. "Should we play that instead?"

"A noob like you wouldn't be much of a challenge." But I knew the offer wasn't serious.

"Down, tiger!" she laughed.

Realistically, a basketball's low *thud* made way too much noise; the teachers would be onto us in seconds flat. Plus, we were still in uniform. In a game that required lots of jumping, we'd both inevitably be distracted by the physics of our skirts. Ping-pong, on the other hand, wasn't quite so strenuous. It was the perfect little game to play up here, away from the rest of the world.

Adachi and I were first-years in high school, and both of us were truant to an extent. We were by no means old friends or anything like that; on the contrary, we'd first met right there on that campus, and our friendship was relatively new. By this point, I knew a fair amount about her, but there was a lot I still didn't know...probably because I didn't *need* to know it.

When it came to her appearance, Adachi typically played it safe. Her hair was on the longer side, with a smattering of bleached streaks that didn't draw too much attention. Her physique was slender, with few curves to speak of, and her shoulders were so slumped that I half-wondered if she even *had* shoulders. With her sharp eyes and thin lips, she had a classic case of "resting bitch face," but actually she was pretty laid-back, or easygoing, or however you want to put it. No matter how angry she got, she never raised her voice...at least, not that I'd ever seen.

She often wore a bracelet on her left wrist—an oversized bangle, reminiscent of a single handcuff, that always looked as though it was trying to slip off.

In contrast to Adachi, my hair was visibly bleached to a tawny copper color, and I put more effort into my makeup. Girls like me got slapped with the "delinquent" label over *one* tiny little piercing, so naturally, the teachers preferred Adachi by a wide margin. Probably because she was a pretty girl who didn't talk back.

Make no mistake, however—Adachi was easily three times the delinquent I was. One look at her attendance record would prove that. But what pissed me off was that, even if I were three times better than her, I would never be seen as a "good" student. Yet, somehow, she still managed to get the same grades as me. It was *baffling*.

Adachi pulled off her uniform jacket and tied it around her waist. Once we'd set the table up, I followed suit—partially because I didn't want to rip my jacket, but mostly because the loft was sweltering. Next, I wiped off my makeup, since I knew all the sweating would just ruin it anyway. Then, cradling a mottled pink ping-pong ball in my palm, I picked up one of the old, probably moldy paddles with my free hand. When Adachi moved to do the same, I realized for the first time that she was left-handed.

"When was the last time you played?" I asked as we batted the ball back and forth.

"Umm...probably sixth grade, in Girl Scouts?"

Girl Scouts. Now *that* brought back memories.

"Oh man, Girl Scouts... Feels like forever ago." I smiled to myself.

As a right-handed player, it was pretty easy for me to aim the ball at Adachi's unguarded right side, so I went for it without the slightest hesitation. In response, Adachi positioned herself firmly dead-center and returned the ball with a skillful backhand drive.

"Whoa... You're pretty good."

"You think *that's* good? Check this out." As the ball bounced weakly toward her, she switched the paddle to her right hand and smashed it back in my direction.

"Holy crap!" My eyes widened. Naturally, the ball went flying past the table and bounced off the net behind me.

And so, we idled away the time playing ping-pong—casual games, for the most part, though we had our moments of intense competition. Meanwhile, the rest of the school sat through third period. *What was third period on Mondays again? Math? History?* I tried to remember, but most of my brainpower was focused on the game. Once again, something had gotten in the way of me caring about school. Story of my life.

To be clear, Adachi and I hadn't randomly decided to start playing hooky together. We started out doing our own separate things—and, frankly, Adachi didn't come to school that often to begin with.

In manga, you always see some kid skipping class up on the roof. But, in real life, no school is stupid enough to leave the roof open to students. Even if they did, what good would that be? If you tried to take a nap, you'd probably wake up with a gnarly sunburn. That's why I always chose the gym loft—a quiet, remote part of the school, tucked away from sunlight and prying eyes. And, one day, Adachi made the same choice I did.

It was right at the start of second semester. When I walked in, Adachi was lounging with her shoes *and* socks off, probably due to the heat. She must've thought I was a teacher at first, because she bolted upright when she saw me, her cute little toes all splayed out. I remember it vividly to this day.

After that, we started hanging out more and more frequently. We didn't schedule it, though. Every now and then, I'd get the feeling she was up in the loft, so I'd come by, and *voil*à, she'd be there.

But Adachi rarely stuck around until the end of the day, so after school, I'd usually hang out with my other two friends. Unlike me, however, those friends of mine were "good kids" through and through. Not only did they faithfully attend class, they copied down notes like it was their job.

Two good kids, two bad kids. On one hand, it felt nice and symmetrical, but on the other hand, it kinda seemed like I couldn't pick a side... That was the sort of thing I idly contemplated as the ping-pong ball bounced leisurely back and forth.

Still, more than anything, I was comfortable. This was my peaceful escape from the misery of reality.

"All right, that's it. It's too *hot*!" Adachi complained, unbuttoning her dress shirt's top button.

I dropped my paddle onto the ping-pong table and walked away. "Yeah, I'm done."

My shirt was damp with sweat, and it clung to my skin. I flapped my sleeve cuff, trying desperately to generate airflow. Then I realized I still held the ping-pong ball. I thought about tossing it from here onto the table, but it was too late. I had a feeling the ball would just bounce off, so I decided against it.

The janitors never came up here, and a layer of dust covered the floor like a wax coating. Obviously, neither of us wanted to sit directly onto the dust, so we used the green net as a tarp and sat on that instead.

"I wish there was a breeze," Adachi muttered, her face flushed from the heat.

Same, I thought, and glared up at the window. I knew

that, if we opened it, someone was bound to notice. Then they'd come up here to close it, and we'd be busted.

"Should we go outside? It's almost lunch anyway."

Adachi had rolled up her sleeves and untucked her shirt. I personally wouldn't have been caught dead wearing my uniform that sloppily. It was kind of off-putting to look at, even if we *were* technically in private. *Next thing you know, she'll be flapping her skirt—yep, there she goes.*

"Have you no shame? You're ruining the school's, uhh...what's it called..."

"Dignity?"

"Yeah, that! Our dignity will never recover!"

"So, what should we do for lunch?" she asked, shooting a glance at me.

Fine, ignore me, I guess.

Logically, it was easier for me to go out and get food for us both, since all it would take for me to look presentable would be to put on my jacket. Adachi, on the other hand, would have to tuck her shirt in, button it, roll her sleeves down, *and* put her jacket on. And, if she could see the state her hair was in, she'd probably want to brush it.

"Let me guess—you want me to fetch you something. Fine, fine."

"I'll go next time."

"Yeah, right. That's what you said *last* time." And the time before that, and the time before that, and the time before that, and the time before that.

But Adachi simply laughed. "Just a Danish and some water, pretty please."

"All right. If they're sold out, I'll grab you whatever."

Adachi only ever drank mineral water. *Maybe that's why she has such clear skin. I'm so jealous... If she got a cut, I bet she'd bleed water, too.*

"Are you going to class after lunch?"

"Probably. What about you? Going home?" I asked, uncrossing my arms and resting my hands on the floor.

"Hmm...well, I'm *definitely* not going to class," she replied nonchalantly.

I'd never actually asked her why she skipped class so often, nor had she ever asked me. We were just two people hanging out, trying to alleviate our boredom with some ping-pong.

I held the ping-pong ball in my palm and gave it a hard flick with my other hand. It bounced across the loft with an airy *tap, tap, tap* until it hit the opposite wall and fell still. The sound was reminiscent of light knocking, as though I stood at the door to Adachi's heart.

"Ping-pong is pretty fun, huh?" she mused, taking off her indoor shoes. I thought back to the look on her face as we played, her brow furrowed as she focused her full attention on the game. It took a lot of concentration, after all.

"Yeah, for sure. I think I prefer that sort of one-on-one competition, like, compared to team sports."

In my last year of junior high, I'd realized that, as fun as basketball was, I just wasn't cut out for it. Part of me always itched to test my skill, and my teammates often complained that I hogged the ball too much. In the end, I knew I wasn't fit to be part of a team.

"You know, it's weird. If we were doing this for gym class, I totally wouldn't want to play."

"Yeah, I can relate. I'd be out of there so fast," Adachi agreed, stretching her arms above her head.

Her elbow made a popping sound, and she let out a groan. *Weird. I guess she has naturally flexible elbows.*

"We have a lot of random stuff in common, huh, Shimamura?"

As she said my name, I narrowed my eyes, though I doubt Adachi noticed. Truth be told, I *hated* my surname. It reminded me of Shimamura Co., the clothing store. Whenever someone said it, it felt like they were calling *me* Shimamura Co. by extension. *If only my name were Shimazaki or something instead.*

As we sat in silence with our legs sprawled, the lunch

bell rang, echoing through the otherwise-empty gym. My stomach rumbled in agreement.

"Well, that was the bell," Adachi said.

"Sure was."

"See you soon." She waved goodbye.

I reluctantly heaved myself to my feet, donned my jacket, and slipped back into my indoor shoes. Once I was sure I had my wallet, I headed for the stairs. After a few steps, I glanced back to see Adachi reaching for her bookbag—probably to get her cell phone—but it was ever so slightly out of reach, so she gave up. *Ugh, relatable.*

"Don't be such a lazybones, you sloth," I told her, despite my internal monologue. I heard her stamp her feet in protest, but by that time, I was already halfway down the stairs.

As for who was listed in her phone's address book, well, that was one of the many things I didn't know. I'd never seen Adachi speak to anyone else at our school...probably because she so seldom showed up in the first place. *We've been hanging out a lot lately—maybe she only comes here to see me. No, that's stupid.*

I was certain that, if I ever said that out loud, she would never come back to the gym loft.

The next day, Adachi once again invited me to play ping-pong; she seemed a bit more eager than she had the day before. Curious, I agreed.

After our ungodly struggle yesterday, table setup went a lot faster this time around.

"Is it cool if I serve?"

"Sure." Today the ball was orange, not pink.

"Hyah!" Adachi shouted as she hit the ball. This was no ordinary serve—she struck the ball's lower half with her paddle at a specific angle, creating a weird curveball effect.

The ball hit the table and bounced back in her direction, but I didn't care about its trajectory. I was so baffled by her melodramatic swing that I missed my chance to hit it back.

"Rrgh," I murmured in frustration. Then I caught a rare, eye-catching glimpse of childish glee on Adachi's face.

"I looked up techniques on the internet last night. But I didn't have a paddle at home to practice with, so I had to use a rice scoop," she explained, twirling her paddle in a show of smug self-satisfaction.

Personally, I was surprised to learn that she cared that much about ping-pong, but I kept this to myself. "That's not fair! You can't serve a curveball to a beginner!"

"Get good, scrub! Hyah!" Striking a weird pose, she served another ball. This time, she must've hit it too low, because it bounced backward and hit the wall behind her. She dashed off to retrieve it, then came back scratching her forehead.

"Truth is, I can only get it to work every one in ten tries," she explained as she showed me how to hit the curveball.

"You've got to be the only person I know who gets *worse* with practice." *At this rate, I think I could beat her with my eyes closed.*

On Adachi's third try, the ball flew off yet again, hitting another table and then the floor. It was her screw-up, but because it fell on my side, *I* was forced to go retrieve it.

Just then, I heard a voice from the ground floor of the gym.

My heart leapt into my throat as I froze in place. The ball bounced off to a corner. I could hear girls' voices coming from downstairs. Meanwhile, Adachi had the same reaction I did. She tiptoed around the ping-pong table, and together, we peeked over the edge of the loft to get a view of the ground floor.

From the looks of it, some girls in our grade were setting up volleyball courts for gym class. I only knew they were in our grade because I spotted my friends,

Hino and Nagafuji, carrying the poles and net. If they walked onto the stage and looked up at the second floor, they would see us... My heart wasn't caught in my throat anymore, but my skin felt as though it was buzzing with static electricity.

Back when we'd just sat around and talked, it was easy to hide from gym intruders. Because of that, I hadn't bothered to memorize the full class schedule. With our hands over our mouths, Adachi and I squatted next to each other, wondering in terror whether someone would notice the tiny *tap, tap, tap* of the runaway ping-pong ball.

"Oh my god, I'm totally freaking out," Adachi whispered with a grin on her face.

Adachi, you bad girl. I elbowed her playfully. "What do we do if someone comes up here?" I asked.

With her hands still over her mouth, she laughed and looked upward.

"We could open the window and jump out."

"What? This is the second floor! We'll break our legs!" I protested. I'd never bothered to check what was directly below that window, so the idea scared me. But that was my fault for taking a joke suggestion so seriously.

Adachi nodded pensively to herself. "I see. So, you're calcium-deficient."

"Oh, screw you!"

Since her comment clearly got to me, though, maybe that was an admission of guilt on my part.

We pressed our backs to the one wall separating us from the buzz of conversation below. Apparently, the teacher hadn't showed up yet, so the students were content to stand around. Hino and Nagafuji didn't know where I went when I skipped class, so they probably had no idea I was in the very same building as them... The thought tickled me.

As Adachi and I crouched in hiding, it started to feel as though we were doing something bad. I mean, we totally were, obviously. But there was something fun about sharing that secret with Adachi. Was I just drunk on the thrill of breaking the rules, or was there something about her specifically? Deep down, I knew the answer, but I decided not to think about it. Meanwhile, the orange ping-pong ball rolled all the way into the corner and fell still.

"Maybe we should start drinking milk at lunch sometimes. You know, so we won't break our legs if we need to make an emergency escape," Adachi suggested, and I couldn't quite tell whether she was joking or not.

Then lunch rolled around, and once again, her "I'll go next time" wasn't true.

By the time school ended for the day, Adachi was already gone, as per usual. She told me that whenever she came home too early, her mom got upset, so I figured she was probably wandering around town somewhere to kill time.

As for me, I went to class after lunch, as I'd done the day before. Then, when the final bell rang, I went with Hino and Nagafuji to the bookstore. Normally I never went there, since it was in the exact opposite direction of my house. Today, however, I was looking for something specific. Since it wasn't my usual genre, I had no idea whether they'd even carry it.

"Well, what do you know?" I mused aloud.

Standing in the sports section, I pulled a ping-pong tactics guide off the shelf. *If Adachi's researching online, then I'll research through books*, I thought. I flipped it over to check the price. "Yikes!" I balked. *Never again will I question the power of the almighty search engine. Soooo much cheaper.*

"Whatcha looking at?"

Hino peered over my shoulder to see what was in my hands. We'd all gone our separate ways when we first walked in, but evidently she was curious to see what I was up to. I already knew it would be too much effort to try to hide the book, so I showed her the cover.

"You're joining the ping-pong team?" She tilted her head, puzzled. *We don't have a ping-pong team, you idiot.*

Hino was something of a plain Jane. Never dyed her hair, never shoplifted, probably never even got into a cat-fight with a girl from another school... Not that I'd done either of the latter two myself. She had big, round eyes, and she was charming in an unsophisticated way—the kind of girl who'd make her own sound effects when she played sports. She was always down for anything; if you asked her to do a backflip, she'd probably give it a try right then and there. Her main hobby was fishing, and she often complained that there were no fellow fishing fans in our class...but I digress.

"So, why ping-pong? Did *Friday Roadshow* do an episode on table tennis or something?"

"No, I wasn't inspired by anything in particular. Just felt like it, that's all," I replied evasively. It was too hard to explain... Okay, no, it wasn't. I just didn't *want* to explain. Without reading a single page, I returned the book to its place on the shelf. I was just going to have to search online like Adachi had. At the same time, though, I could imagine her teasing me for "copying her," and that made me mad. So mad, in fact, that it would be really awkward if she *didn't* tease me for it.

"Heyyyy! Don't leave meeee!" called Nagafuji in a

flat, unconvincing voice, demanding our attention as she toddled over to Hino and me.

Big breasts and glasses. That was all you really needed to know about Nagafuji. Her hair was silky and perfectly straight—very fun to play with. When she wasn't in her school uniform, she usually wore it down, letting it rest atop her chest. Not only was she *physically* mature, she had a mature personality to match...though she was also kind of stupid.

"So, what were you guys talking about?"

"Don't worry about it," said Hino, slapping Nagafuji on the boob.

"Okay, then, I won't," Nagafuji replied, smacking Hino over the head.

Supposedly, Hino and Nagafuji had been friends since junior high. But I'd only just met them in high school, so their friendship with me was a little more restrained. Still, friendship wasn't the sort of thing you could force your way into. Try to get too close, and the other person might push you away. Then everything would get complicated.

"That was sexual harassment, and you know it. Explain yourself."

"I realize you're self-conscious about your body, so I figured I'd help you feel more comfortable," Hino replied cheerfully, as though she'd done absolutely nothing wrong. In fact, I'd never once seen her apologize for her antics. *She must have a strong sense of self. Or maybe she's just an ass.*

"You're self-conscious?" I asked Nagafuji.

She looked away shyly, then nodded. "When you have big boobs, the boys tend to stare. So, yeah...I can't help but feel a little self-conscious." She folded her arms over her chest, which, naturally, did absolutely nothing to hide it.

"I bet the guys in our class have all fantasized about touching them," I replied.

"Ewww...that's kinda gross," Nagafuji scoffed, recoiling.

Honestly, they'd probably imagined a lot worse. I didn't want to get raunchy in the middle of a bookstore, though, so I kept it classy. Glancing back at the ping-pong book, I sighed.

"That's just the price you have to pay for being so popular," Hino joked, slapping Nagafuji's boob the same way one would clap their friend on the back. "Oops, my hand sli—aagh!"

In return, Nagafuji smacked her hard over the head.

I sidestepped away from the spectacle so I wouldn't be associated with them.

In the end, we left the store as a trio. Trust me, I could never truly escape those two.

"You sure skip class a lot, Shimamura. What do you do with your time?" Hino asked as she walked beside me, carrying her newly purchased magazine in a plastic bag. Nagafuji turned to look at me as well. For a couple of goody-goodies, they were awfully curious about the life of a truant student.

Unfortunately for them, I had no real story to tell. My lifestyle wasn't so appealing that it would lure my friends away from a life of dutifully battling their drowsiness in class. So, what attracted *me* to it? No idea.

"Oh, I just lounge around. Sometimes I sleep, or stare into space, or play on my phone..." *Or play ping-pong. But I'll keep that last one to myself.*

"Must be nice," Hino commented, though she didn't actually sound jealous at all.

"And you do it on campus? I should think a teacher would find you sooner or later," Nagafuji remarked, baffled. She was a good girl who only went where she was supposed to, so it was natural that she couldn't think of a hiding spot. And I didn't particularly want to corrupt her or Hino.

"Oh! I bet I know where you go!" Hino declared suddenly.

"Huh?" My eyes widened. I knew she was probably bluffing, but still.

"How about we go looking for her next time she cuts class?" Nagafuji suggested brightly to Hino.

"Please don't," I replied, half-joking, half-exasperated. I really didn't want them to find me. More specifically, I wasn't sure that Adachi would want them to find us together.

"Oh, yeah, that reminds me. Last Sunday, I was at the fishing hole, and I met this total weirdo!" Hino announced proudly for some reason.

"So what? You meet weirdos all the time." *Why does she always think it's some sort of accomplishment?*

Inevitably, anyone Hino ever introduced me to turned out to be an oddball. It was bizarre, actually.

Does she have some sort of natural weirdo magnetism? In that case, would that make me a weirdo, too?

"Better a weirdo than a pervert," Nagafuji remarked. *Okay, but just because it could be worse doesn't make it good.*

"This time, it was a kid wearing, like, a *space suit*-looking thing!" Hino exclaimed gleefully. *As long as you're happy, I guess.*

As Hino regaled us with the story of how she met the newest addition to her weirdo collection, we walked all the way back to the school. From there, we would go our separate ways home. Hino and Nagafuji both took the bus, so I would walk them to the bus stop, then go the rest of the way home on my own.

My family *did* own a bike, but I rarely got the chance to use it myself, since my mom needed it to get to work. She was the super-athletic gym-bunny type, and she pedaled at such inhuman speeds that she directly inspired at least one urban legend in our town.

Just as we passed the gas station, Hino pointed ahead of us. "Look!"

Once we turned in the direction she was pointing, she lowered her arm. Then I saw it.

"Oh."

It was Adachi.

People weren't really supposed to sit on the fence separating the pedestrian walkway from the cars. But there she was, jacket off and shirt untucked in her usual sloppy fashion, adjusting her bangs in a compact mirror. In this instance, I wasn't worried about decorum so much as her personal safety. If she lost her balance and fell backward, she'd land in the middle of traffic.

Next to her was a blue bicycle. That was the moment I learned that Adachi rode a bike to school.

Then she spotted us.

33

"Gah!" Hino squeaked in mild fright. I strongly doubted that she or Nagafuji had ever held a conversation with Adachi, and they weren't aware that I was friends with her. So, for all they knew, some random delinquent was giving them the stink-eye. I needed to factor that into my next move.

So...what *was* my next move? Truth be told, I hadn't given much thought to the possibility that I'd encounter Adachi outside the gym loft. How was I meant to react? I could see her looking at me, but I hesitated to interact further. She seemed hesitant, too.

Still, I knew we couldn't keep staring awkwardly at each other, so...I looked away. I chose to act like I didn't know her. As we passed Adachi, I tried my best to pretend she wasn't there—not even a hello.

Was she mad at me for doing that? I glanced back to check, and our eyes met again, so I averted my gaze. *Oh my god, why is this so awkward?* It felt like we were a couple of twelve-year-olds trying to hide our relationship from the rest of the school... Then again, I suppose that, in a sense, we kind of were.

"Who *was* that? Wasn't she in our class back in, like, April?" Nagafuji asked me, tucking a strand of hair behind her ear. *Oh, for crying out loud.*

"You ask this same question every time we see her," Hino sighed.

"Do I?" She tilted her head, puzzled. Like I said, Nagafuji was kind of stupid.

"Her name is Adachi," I explained for the umpteenth time. "She's in our grade."

"And she's a delinquent with a capital D. According to the teachers, anyway," Hino added, stating the obvious. *Who else would decide that, if not the teachers?*

"Delinquent, huh? Friend of yours, Shimamura?"

"No comment."

In Nagafuji's eyes, I was in the same category as Adachi. To her, the only difference was that I sometimes attended class, whereas Adachi did not. There were no "good" bad students. No gray areas.

But Adachi and I were different in one critical way. Although she was a delinquent through and through, I was really only an underachiever. Like an iguana, wasting my day sleeping in a sunbeam. Just plain lazy.

So, what was a delinquent like Adachi doing, sitting out there?

I glanced back a second time, but by then, she had already taken off on her bike.

The next day was a Wednesday—sadly, the week was only halfway over. Adachi didn't turn up in the loft that morning, though. First period started, and some class that wasn't mine filed into the building for gym. Then the bell rang, and they left. Still no sign of Adachi.

The cloudy weather reduced the light (and heat) that filtered through the second-floor window, creating the perfect climate in which to zone out. But despite my love of staring into space, I started to get bored by the time third period rolled around.

Once it was clear that no one was coming to the gym for third period, I grabbed a ping-pong paddle and retrieved the orange ball that had wandered into the corner yesterday. There, I bounced it against the wall, and when it bounced back, I hit it again—like I was playing wallball or whatever it's called.

I wanted to get some practice in so I could stay ahead of Adachi. Not that I really needed to, since that "special move" she taught herself only seemed to make her worse. But, as I played, I kept glancing furtively at the stairs. When was she going to show up? I'd gotten used to seeing her every day, so her absence unsettled me.

After the incident the day before, I was kind of worried. I mean, I was probably just overthinking it, but still. What if she stopped coming to the loft over the encounter? I would regret it for the rest of...maybe not my *life*, but the semester, at the very least. Once the next semester started, I'd be in a new class, and the old memories would fade.

I'd said goodbyes to lots of different people over the course of my life thus far, but those were all in the past. Now I had Adachi and Hino and Nagafuji.

To me, socializing was like slowly sinking to the bottom of a deep, deep ocean...until eventually you couldn't take it anymore, and had to come up for air.

"Oh!"

I heard someone coming up the stairs, so I caught the ball and waited to find out who. You'd think I would have been nervous that it was a teacher, but I could tell from the sound of the intruder's footsteps that they were wearing a student's indoor shoes.

Sure enough, who should appear at the top of the stairs but Adachi herself. She took one look at me and smiled with relief. The only thing unusual about her was that she hadn't brought her bookbag.

"Hey there. Running late this morning or what?" I asked.

"Oh, no. Actually, I was considering taking off, but I thought I'd stop by on my way out," she replied, brushing her hair out of her face.

Leaving already? But it's not even lunch... Wait, does that mean she was somewhere on campus the whole time?

"Plus, I heard you playing ping-pong," she continued, eyeing the ball and paddle in my hands as she took her seat in the usual spot.

She heard me? From where? Is it really that loud?

I returned the ping-pong equipment to the table, then joined her on the floor. After a moment, I turned to her. "So, I saw you yesterday."

"You sure did," she nodded.

The vibe between us felt a little awkward. Kind of like when you're a kid, and you see your teacher in a restaurant or something, and you realize for the first time that they have an entire life outside school.

For some reason, long silences were oddly common in my interactions with Adachi. Maybe that was because I hadn't quite decided how much emotional investment to put into the relationship. After all, I was free to call Adachi my friend if I wanted, but that didn't mean anything unless the feeling was mutual.

"Where's your bag?"

"With my bike. I didn't feel like bringing it."

She didn't seem to have her phone or wallet, either. Evidently, she really didn't plan to stick around. I was tempted to warn her that her stuff might get stolen,

38

but I could already hear her response: *"What are you, my mom?"*

"So, you ride your bike to school? I didn't know that."

"Really? Haven't you seen me swinging my bike key around?" She pulled her keyring out of her pocket to demonstrate. Attached to the keyring was a keychain of a purple...dog? Cow? Some sort of four-legged animal.

"Okay, now I remember. I guess I didn't stop to think about it."

There was a lull in the conversation. We surely had more to talk about, yet nothing was coming to mind. Adachi must've felt the same way; she looked up at the window on the other side of the loft and smiled. "Well... Guess I'll go." She got to her feet.

"Oh... Okay," I nodded, looking up at her. She dusted off the back of her skirt and headed for the stairs, swinging her key again. *Already? That was fast. What did she even come up here for? Just to say hi, I guess?*

"Hey, um... Adachi?" I called from the floor.

"Hmm?" Curious, she turned back.

"If you had to either go to class with me or walk home with me, which would you choose?"

Why did I just ask her that? I didn't know.

Deep down on the inside, I was riddled with holes. Holes where my heart should have been. Maybe it was just my empty stomach talking, but right then, the holes were screaming at me, telling me that something was missing.

At first, Adachi looked at me in mild surprise...but it didn't take her long to find an answer.

"Okay then. I'll kill time somewhere until school ends."

Naturally, she chose the second option. *I should've known she wouldn't choose class. That was a stupid question.* I grinned.

"Meet you at the same place as yesterday?" she asked.

"Sure thing," I answered.

She waved goodbye, so I waved back, a bit less enthusiastically.

The idea of her returning to school expressly to walk home with me felt kind of silly—okay, *really* silly—but kind of funny, too. So, with excitement budding in my chest, I saw Adachi off with a smile.

Looking forward to the end of the school day was a frequent occurrence for me. Today in particular, however, that feeling had shot up 20 percent.

When Nagafuji had club activities to attend, the clubless Hino and I often went home by ourselves. But today,

I had "other business," so I bid Hino goodbye and left her standing alone at the shoe lockers.

"Noooo! My inner pet rabbit is gonna starve!" she wailed...whatever that was supposed to mean.

The best thing about Hino and Nagafuji? They didn't try to "reform" me or get involved in my life. At most, they might voice their disapproval. Otherwise, they were content to let me be.

Slipping my outdoor shoes on, I walked outside into drizzling rain. *Oh, crap. I didn't bring an umbrella.* I started walking faster, and by the time I reached the school gates, I had broken into a run. Was Adachi out here waiting for me? Truth be told, I felt so guilty, I probably would've run regardless of the weather. Not out of excitement or anything. Just to be polite.

I shot past a group of guys in school uniforms. Just as I passed the gas station, Adachi came into view. My guilt was still there, but now I felt oddly relieved, too. There she was, waiting patiently with an umbrella over her head. I was admittedly surprised that she'd brought one.

"You didn't have to sit in the exact same place!" I laughed, slightly out of breath as I jogged over. She perched on the fence once again; when she saw me, she hopped down and grabbed her bike's handlebars. I came to a stop right next to her.

Whew... Made it, I thought, even though we weren't even one-tenth of the way to my house yet.

"Hey! Sorry about the rain."

"Nah, it's fine. Not like you can control the weather," she grinned. "Here, hold this."

At her request, I took the umbrella. With her hands free, she hopped onto her bike, kicked up the kickstand, and glanced back at me.

"Which way is your house?"

I pointed straight down the road.

"Ah. Figured."

Her expression clouded over, as though she was disappointed. I fixed her with an inquiring look.

"Oh, it's just a pretty big detour from my house, that's all." She pointed in a 70-degree angle from where I'd indicated. I wasn't surprised to learn that she lived pretty far away from me, since otherwise we would've gone to the same junior high school. *Wait, but then...why did she go out of her way to hang out on this street yesterday, if it's so far from her house?* There was just so much I still didn't know about her.

"Which way should we go first?"

"Now there's a bold question. Uhhh...why don't we go to your house?" I answered. No matter whose house we stopped at first, the other person would have a long trek

42

alone ahead of them, and I didn't want to inconvenience Adachi more than I already had.

She didn't argue. Instead, she climbed onto her bike. "Wanna ride on the back?" she offered, tapping the rear wheel with her foot. "You can hold the umbrella for us."

That sounded like a perfectly reasonable idea to me, but I decided to tease her anyway. "We're not *supposed* to ride double, you know."

"We're delinquents, remember? We do all kinds of stuff we're not supposed to."

"Oh, right. Well then, good thing we're not honor students!"

"Amen to that."

Without further ado, I hopped on, placing my feet on either side of the rear wheel and putting one hand on Adachi's shoulder. With my free hand, I held the umbrella aloft. "Okay, I'm ready."

Once I was in position, she started to pedal. In the beginning, she struggled with the added weight, but as the bike steadily picked up speed, she seemed to find her groove.

I looked down at the top of her head. Normally I only saw her hair as it framed her face, so the view from up there was kind of surreal. Her hair almost looked like a small, shaggy animal. *I wonder if my hair looks like that from this angle, too.*

If one of us were a goody-goody, this would've been the perfect moment in our friendship for the good kid to try to lead the bad kid back onto the "proper" path. But we were both bad kids, so it wasn't. If anything, we were both dragging each other further down.

Also, the umbrella was too high up to actually shield either of us from the rain.

"I didn't know you had friends, Shimamura," Adachi commented, her eyes on the road as we went back the way I'd come. Her tone was casual, if a little dry, or maybe it just sounded that way from above. Either way, for some reason, I felt like things could get awkward depending on how I responded.

"Yeah, you know... Can't have Shimamura without Uniqlo and H&M," I joked, even though I hated my stupid last name. Then I felt Adachi's shoulders shake, and knew she was laughing.

"I thought you only skipped class because you were lonely?"

It wasn't often that she asked me questions about myself. Or maybe the fact that I felt that way said more about me than about her...so I decided to ask her something in return.

"What about you? Any friends?"

"Mmm...just you, really."

"Wow, that's pretty sad." But, actually, I was kind of happy to hear it. Not that it was a good thing...at least, not for Adachi.

We took a sharp turn around a corner, and for some reason—possibly my added weight—that simple movement made the bike lose its balance and nearly graze the side of a building. Once Adachi got the bike back under control, she took her eyes off the road and looked up at me instead.

"Wh-what?"

She didn't respond right away—just kept pedaling, her upper body tilted in my direction. Common sense told me that at least one of us needed to watch where we were going, and yet I couldn't tear my gaze away from hers.

"You know, when you were jogging over to me, I noticed something."

"Yeah...?"

"You're kind of catlike, aren't you?"

I could hear the faint whirring of the bicycle tires beneath us.

"Catlike?"

"As in, not human."

Wow, rude. Do I run weird or something? Or is it my face? Do I have a catlike face?

"How so?"

"You're just so aloof with people."

"I am...?"

"I think so." *Because you never try to connect with some-one on a personal level,* her eyes seemed to say. My fingers tightened around her shoulder.

I could admit that I wasn't a total open book, but surely *everyone* was like that to an extent, right? Or... perhaps the fact that I saw that as normal was the exact reason she considered me "aloof" to begin with. Even so, wasn't she the same way?

Then again, I'd never owned a cat, so I couldn't say for sure one way or the other.

"If I'm 'so aloof with people,' then what am I doing sharing a bike with you, hmm?"

"Maybe you see me as a fellow cat," she replied, and finally turned back to face the road.

I should have felt relieved that we were back to operating under safe conditions, but all I felt was unease. I *really* didn't like talking about myself. My mind evaded the topic by turning to the subject of Adachi instead. Was she "catlike," too? Were we just a couple of cats, lounging in a sunbeam up in the gym loft?

The way we'd swatted eagerly at those ping-pong balls, I could certainly see a resemblance.

"I don't know how to get back to the school from here," I said. "Draw me a map."

"Oh, right. Duh."

Clearly, I hadn't thought this through. Nevertheless, Adachi easily complied with my demand; she reached into her bookbag and retrieved a notebook and pen. I half-expected them to be covered in dust, given how often she attended class. In fact, it was a miracle that she bothered to bring her bookbag at all.

When we arrived at Adachi's house thirty or so minutes later, I noticed that it was really white. The walls, I mean. There was a covered parking space on the left-hand side, but no car was parked there. I also glimpsed a green clothesline pole peeking out from around the side of the house.

Across from the front of the house was a long stretch of farmland—three or four different plots, all in a row. Beyond them was a single giant building...probably a mill, if I had to guess. The area around my house was like this, too. Everything about it screamed rural backwater town.

In the past, there had been a lot more farmland, and houses were scarce. The smell of grass had followed you everywhere you went. But now, as the residential areas expanded, that farmland was shrinking. In grade school, I'd once drawn a picture of the roadside farms I passed on my walk to and from school; today, that landscape didn't exist anymore.

"Okay, all done," said Adachi. "This is the path I take to school on my bike, so in theory, you should be fine."

"*In theory?* What's that supposed to mean? You think I'm wider than a bike?"

"Well, I mean, if you stuck your arms out!" Adachi laughed.

She tore the map out of her notebook, then handed it to me.

Why would I stretch out my arms all the way back to school, you idiot?

I looked down at the map and traced the path with my finger. Quietly, I realized that this "map to school" also served as a map to Adachi's *house*. Not that I saw myself visiting anytime soon, of course. What if I showed up, and she wasn't home? Talk about awkward.

"How damp are you?" Adachi touched my shoulder, then my hair. "Jeez, you're soaked!"

"Yeah, it started coming down harder on our way here."

Adachi's hair was likewise so wet that her bangs were glued to her forehead. She realized what I was looking at and raked her fingers through her hair, slicking it back and exposing her forehead. This new "hairstyle" gave her a slightly more mature vibe.

"Wanna come inside and towel off?"

"Mmm...I'm good. You wouldn't want me to drip all over your house, right?"

It felt as though I was asking her to give me a reason to decline. She sighed and rolled her eyes. "There you go again, keeping people at arm's length."

It pissed me off that she assumed that, and it made me want to lash out. Not very healthy, I know.

"Okay, then I guess I'll come in."

"You *guess*? Ugh, just go home."

Exactly when I finally agree, you change your mind? Wow, rude. Fine, whatever. I wasn't that attached to the idea, anyway.

But, right as I turned to leave, she stopped me.

"Wait, Shimamura. Here." She handed me the folding umbrella we'd used on our way to her house. "You're going to need this, don't you think?"

"Yeah, probably. I'll give it back to you tomorrow, I promise."

"*If* I go to school tomorrow, sure."

Classic Adachi. Since my hands were full, I waved the umbrella at her, then started walking.

It had taken us thirty minutes to get there by bike; assuming my added weight slowed Adachi down, I estimated that it normally took her about twenty minutes. My walking speed was maybe half that, so I was looking at a forty-minute walk. And that was just to get back to the school. From there, it would take me another twenty minutes to get home. Total ETA: one hour.

"Ugh... This is gonna suck..."

"Shimamura!"

I heard Adachi's voice from somewhere above me and looked upward to find her peeking out of a second-floor window. Apparently, she'd run all the way up there. *What a dork,* I thought to myself with a chuckle.

"What's up?"

"Oh, um... First things first, here's a hand towel for you!"

With that, she flung the towel from the window. Desperate to catch it before it hit the wet ground, I dropped the umbrella and held out both hands.

"Why would you do that...?" I heard her mutter in disbelief. *Whatever. At least, this way, I managed to catch it.* I grabbed the umbrella off the ground and started wiping my face.

The hand towel was lemon yellow. It must have been freshly washed, too, because it didn't smell like Adachi. Not that I needed it to.

"Thanks!"

"No problem."

There was a long moment of silence. Adachi had prefaced the towel with "first things first," so I looked up at her, waiting for whatever else she had to say. But she simply stared back, resting her elbows on the windowsill with her chin in her hands. The only sound was the pouring rain.

Meanwhile, as I patted my hair dry, I contemplated returning the towel to Adachi tomorrow as well.

Then, finally, she spoke. "Sorry."

"Huh? For what?"

"For making you walk all that way. I feel bad," she explained, though she certainly wasn't showing it on her face if so. "Should I just take you home?"

"What? No, no, no. Then you'd just have to bike all the way back."

Why had I wanted to come here? I sincerely didn't know.

"Oh, right. I guess that makes sense," Adachi nodded, her expression steely.

Another moment of silence.

The empty space between her and me drove me *bonkers*. I was torn between the urge to say something—anything—and the desire to flee. Since I couldn't think of anything to say, I chose the latter.

"Well, I'd better go. See you."

"Yeah, see you tomorrow...probably."

If. Probably. She refused to commit, right to the very end.

Once she closed the window, I turned and headed off, towel draped around my neck as though I were a middle-aged man.

"What a weird day."

As I carefully followed the path outlined on the map, I thought about Adachi. Why would she bother biking twenty minutes to school if she wasn't going to attend class?

Today we'd talked about friends. *Maybe, next time, I should ask her about school.*

"And so, Adachi-san turned up at school the next day like it was the most natural thing in the world."

"I know, right? I'm gonna make honor roll at this rate."

Give me a break, I thought, shooting Adachi an icy look as I hit the ping-pong ball back in her direction.

To us, today was just another Wednesday. Morning classes had passed, and when the bell rang, I contemplated buying lunch for the two of us after this game ended. But then I heard footsteps, and two cheerful voices entered the gym.

They were headed for the loft.

"I'm telling you, there were sounds coming from up here," a painfully familiar voice explained as two pairs of feet thudded up the stairs. When they reached the landing, I grimaced in spite of myself.

"Ugh..."

"Excuse me? Your friends are here to see you, and your first reaction is *ugh*?"

Carrying plastic bags from the school store, Hino and Nagafuji started to walk over to me...but then they saw Adachi and froze in their tracks.

"Nngh..." Hino looked at me and Adachi in turn. Then Adachi looked at me. *Everyone* was looking at me. *God, I wish I could disappear right now.*

But I couldn't, obviously. So, instead, I set my ping-pong paddle on the table and sat down in my usual spot.

"You're awfully calm about all this," Hino snarked. Regardless, she plopped down next to me, and Nagafuji took a seat on my opposite side. Meanwhile, Adachi remained standing, fiddling with a strand of hair. I beckoned her over, but she scratched her head and frowned.

"Come *on*, Adachi," I insisted.

At that, she finally caved. With a reluctant grimace, she walked over and sat a short distance from the rest of us, since Nagafuji was in her usual spot.

"How did you find me?" I asked Hino.

"I remembered that you were looking at a ping-pong book in the bookstore, so I kinda put two and two together."

"Oops." So, it was my fault, then. Feeling guilty, I glanced at Adachi out of the corner of my eye. She observed us with her usual steely expression, and I got the distinct sense that she had no intention of joining the conversation.

Hino tugged on my sleeve and whispered, "Is that Adachi-san?"

She's right there, you know. You could just ask her.

"I think the answer is obvious, but yeah."

"Oh, right! Adachi-san!" Nagafuji nodded. *What, did you forget her name AGAIN?*

"So, you guys *are* friends!"

"Yeah, I guess." *Can't exactly play it off this time.*

Hino tilted her head in confusion. "But then, why—well, okay." Partway through her question, she seemed to change her mind.

Nagafuji glanced at her, then turned to Adachi. "My name's Nagafuji."

"And I'm Hino. Nice to meet you, ma'am," Hino chimed in.

Ma'am? Dude, she's the same age as us. You KNOW this.

Adachi pointed at each of them in turn. "Nagafuji and Hino. I'll remember that."

At this, Hino shrank back a little. *Why did you have to phrase it so ominously?*

"Nice to meet you," Adachi finished curtly, then leaned back against the net and stared silently at the opposite wall. She radiated such an intense "stay away" vibe that neither Hino nor Nagafuji had the courage to engage with her.

Instead, they both turned to me.

"Oh yeah, we bought some stuff for lunch. Figured we could eat together."

"So, the teachers never come up here? Even during gym class? That's amazing."

I just wish they wouldn't both talk at the same time. How am I supposed to know who to respond to first? Guess I'll start with the food.

I reached into the plastic bag Hino held and pulled out the first sandwich I came into contact with. "Thanks," I told her, and took a couple bites. Then, at last, I answered Nagafuji's question. "Whenever there's a gym class, we just sit quietly so they don't spot us."

"Incredible! Either they're all a bunch of blind idiots, or they just don't care!" Nagafuji exclaimed in awe. Personally, I was impressed that she managed to insult people in that upbeat tone—a contrast so glaring, it was practically perpendicular. Unlike her chest, which was more of a bell curve. But I digress.

"What kind do you want, Adachi?" I asked, shifting the conversation to her.

"Whichever kind you like is fine," she replied without moving an inch.

"Hmm...okay, then, here you go." I gently tossed her an egg sandwich.

"Thanks," she said to no one in particular.

Meanwhile, Nagafuji and Hino each took a sandwich and a drink and started eating. They chatted mostly with each other, and occasionally with me, but never spoke directly to Adachi. Adachi showed no interest in talking to them, either. The atmosphere between the three was so strained and uncomfortable, the bread in my mouth felt like sandpaper. This was a game of tug-of-war, and I was the rope. *This really isn't helping my digestion.*

Once Hino finished eating, her boredom soon got the best of her. "Can we play ping-pong? C'mon, let's play!" she exclaimed, tugging on my arm.

I glanced at Adachi and hesitated. "We're still eating, though. Maybe after."

But, when I looked over, I realized that Nagafuji had already finished her food. *Are Adachi and I slow eaters or something?*

"Okay then... Nagafuji! Play with me!"

"Fine by me. What are we betting?"

"What? We have to bet something?"

Hino and Nagafuji walked over and grabbed the ball and paddles Adachi and I had been using. As I watched them, suddenly something felt *wrong*. I just wasn't sure what.

"Hey, Shimamura, are you free Saturday?" Hino asked as they played.

"This Saturday?"

"Yeah, this—*Saturday*—!" Hino grunted as she lunged for the ball. She knocked it back to Nagafuji, who swatted it even harder.

"Sure, I'm not doing anything."

"In that case, you should come meet my little astronaut friend! The kid's a hoot!"

"So, what you're really saying is, you want me to go fishing with you?"

"No! I mean, yeah, but that's just a bonus, if anything! See, I told 'em all about you, and now they wanna meet you!"

Oh god, what did you tell them? My life was perfectly uneventful, so what could possibly interest this weirdo? Or was Hino just joking? She was so engrossed in the ping-pong game, it was hard to get a read on her.

"Why not take Nagafuji?"

"I've got *club activities*," Nagafuji replied, in a tone that seemed to say, "Unlike you losers, I actually have a LIFE." If you asked me, club activities didn't seem that much more important than going fishing, but whatever.

"So, there you have it! Let's go fishing, Shimamura!"

"Hmm...eh, okay. Saturday it is."

"Rock and roll!" Hino shouted as she swung her paddle hard—and missed.

Once there was a lull in the conversation, I glanced at Adachi. She stared into space, holding her half-eaten sandwich. We were both the quiet type, so whenever someone else talked, we were content to simply listen. But she wasn't looking at Hino and me, so I knew something else was going on.

And, whatever it was, it wasn't good.

The next day was a Friday—my favorite day of the week, since it meant the weekend was right around the corner. Once again, as on Wednesday, Adachi didn't turn up at the loft. After yesterday, however, I had seen that coming. Somehow, I knew Hino and Nagafuji's presence would deter Adachi from hanging out up here.

I got the feeling that no amount of waiting around would help me this time. Maybe Adachi would never come back to the loft ever again. And if she stopped coming up here, then we would pretty much stop hanging out completely. Worst-case scenario, it was possible that I wouldn't see her again until graduation.

"Worst-case scenario, huh...?"

In other words, my ideal scenario was to keep hanging out with her. I *wanted* to see her. Nothing weird about that, obviously, since we were friends and all. It would've been weirder if I *didn't* want to hang out with her. Especially considering how often we met up in the loft. Clearly, we enjoyed each other's company. Nothing wrong with that.

But whatever was between the two of us evaporated into thin air with the addition of Hino and Nagafuji.

It's because Adachi's so shifty—no, that's not it. There's a better way to put it, but I just can't think of it at the moment. Yeah, that's the reason she's so quick to start avoiding me.

I grasped the concept on an intuitive level, but I couldn't describe it in words. The feeling was exasperating.

Sometimes it really, really bothered me just how little I knew about her. Instead, all I really understood was myself, and even then, not a whole lot.

Yesterday, when I had watched Hino and Nagafuji play ping-pong, I realized: *This is not what I want.* I didn't want all four of us to get together and start a big, happy ping-pong team. No track suits, no training montage. All I wanted—all I came to the loft for—was to laze around in my school uniform and enjoy the unique, peaceful lethargy that only existed between Adachi and me.

At least, I THINK that's what I want.

Granted, I hadn't arrived at the root of the problem just yet.

So far, all I knew for sure was that some part of me viscerally opposed Hino and Nagafuji coming up here.

"We're meeting up at 10:00 tomorrow morning, got it? If you're late, I won't help you bait your hook!"

"I hear you, I hear you."

I still wasn't sure that I wanted to go fishing just so I could meet some spaceman weirdo, but whatever. Shrugging off Hino's warning, I left the classroom. Today

I had declined to hang out with her and Nagafuji in favor of going home alone.

As I walked down the hallway, down the stairs, and to the shoe lockers, I stared at the map to Adachi's house and contemplated paying her a visit. Ultimately, however, I decided against that. Somehow, I doubted I'd find her sitting around at home.

Going through the school's front gates, I turned and walked down the street. As I passed the gas station, a tiny part of me hoped I'd find Adachi waiting for me on the fence again, and my pace quickened. Sadly, no such luck. All I found was an empty fence.

As an experiment, I tried sitting on the fence the same way Adachi did, with one leg up. I almost fell backward into traffic. *Okay, no more of that.*

Nursing my wounded ego, I slowed my pace as I continued down the street. For a moment, I thought about going into the gas station convenience store, then decided against it. Instead, I cut across the deserted parking lot outside the optician's shop. I took a left at the cram school in the green cylindrical building, and a right as I passed the bus stop where Hino, Nagafuji, and I typically went our separate ways.

"BAM!"

"Gah!"

Someone bumped into me from behind, and I stumbled forward. At first I braced myself, thinking that maybe it was some delinquent creep about to harass me for money. Then I turned around and discovered that I was at least partially right. The delinquent part, anyway.

It was Adachi. Apparently, she had reached out from atop her bike and shoved me. I was just grateful that she hadn't slammed her whole bike into me.

"Sorry about that. I didn't hit the brakes in time."

"Says the girl who shouted 'BAM!' as she was doing it."

She hopped off her bike and walked next to me, pushing it along. I hadn't seen her at school that day, but she was wearing her uniform, and her bookbag sat in her bike basket. Next to it was a plastic bag from god-knows-where.

I started walking again, and she followed along.

"You sure?"

"About what?"

"Walking with me. It's a pretty big detour from your house, remember?"

"Yeah...I guess it is."

She tilted her head down toward the ground, but kept walking. Maybe she wanted to go to my house, since we'd gone to hers last time. Or maybe she was just trying to kill time.

As we walked in silence, I snuck a few glances at her. In profile, her hair lay perfectly against her high cheekbones, as though she were a carefully crafted statue. After a moment, she blinked, and I was relieved to remember that she was a living, breathing human being. Then our eyes met, and I realized I'd been staring for too long.

She grabbed the plastic bag out of the bike basket and offered it to me.

"Here. This is for you."

"Huh? What is it?"

I peered inside to find two buns, one of which I recognized as cream bun-shaped. The other was shaped like a tartlet with something white on top—tuna or mashed potatoes, I couldn't really tell. The school store sold both buns. There was also a bottle of mineral water at the bottom of the bag, but it had clearly been in there for a while, because it wasn't remotely cold. This seemed like a lot of food for breakfast, yet not quite enough for a decent lunch.

"I meant to give this to you at lunch today," she said.

"Lunch?"

I tried to picture Adachi standing in line in the middle of the busy cafeteria, but couldn't. *No way.* Then I realized what she meant.

"*Ohhh*, I get it. It was finally your turn today, huh?"

This was the first smile I'd managed to get out of her today. The sunset's gentle rays offset her sharp gaze.

"How much was it? I'll pay you back."

I moved to get my wallet out.

"Don't worry about it," she replied evasively.

If she wouldn't tell me the cost herself, I was going to have to work it out from memory. The mineral water was easy, assuming she bought it from the school vending machine. I just needed to remember the price of the tartlet.

"Rrgh..." I furrowed my brow in intense contemplation.

"What's the matter with you?" Adachi asked dubiously.

I ignored her and focused all my energy into digging through my memory bank. *Right* before I was about to pass out, I finally remembered. I took out my wallet and checked the cash I had on hand. *Perfect.* I removed the exact amount and handed it to her.

"This is for the tartlet and the water. I bet I got it exactly right, didn't I?" I demanded smugly.

Adachi simply tilted her head in puzzlement. "Actually, I'm not sure. I can't remember how much it cost."

"Ugh. You're no fun."

Disappointed, I cracked open the water bottle and took a swig. The lukewarm water tasted like the last dregs of a bygone summer. Personally, I'd wasted that summer just lying around.

Once I slaked my thirst, I offered her a sip.

"Want some?"

She took the bottle and chugged about a third of its contents. When she finally pulled away, she heaved a sigh of relief, staring out at the road ahead of us.

"I'm so glad you didn't walk home with your other friends. I would've missed my chance to give it to you."

Why would that have stopped you? I wondered. I almost said it aloud, too. But then, I saw something in her expression, and realized the best way to describe her was *childish*. With her averted gaze and pout, she looked exactly like a little kid throwing a silent tantrum. She wasn't "shifty"—she was *sulky*. I'd gotten the two words mixed up because they sounded alike.

Wait, did they? Or was that just me?

Anyway.

If I were Adachi's only friend—and, according to her, I was—then clearly she was jealous. Obviously I couldn't say that to her face; she'd just get mad and deny it. Maybe she'd take off and go home without me.

Frankly, I was just as embarrassed about it as she was. It took a lot of courage just to look at her. But, despite the emotional agony, I pressed on. It was time to set things straight—one thing, at least.

"Adachi?"

She looked at me. Holding her gaze firmly, I pointed down the street.

"You're coming with me to my house, right?"

It was the most I could ask...and, if I had to guess, probably the most she could agree to. At least, for now. I'd need a lot more practice if I wanted to put a new spin on the ping-pong ball bouncing back and forth between us.

"Yeah, that's the plan," she answered.

"Cool." I smiled.

Swinging the plastic bag in my hand, it occurred to me that I'd need to draw Adachi a map.

And so, the four of us formed a weird, tentative connection. But this wasn't a happy, harmonious circle; it was a deformed lump with me at the center.

Would Adachi ever happily agree to go fishing with Hino? I had no way of knowing what the future held. My best guess was "probably not," but nevertheless, a small part of me held out hope...and that, in turn, gave wing to faint excitement.

"Look at me! I'm an airplane! Vrrrrmmm!"

I held my arms out to my sides and wondered how many steps I could take before shame kicked in.

2. Fishing for the Future

"**O**OH, CLASSIC! Truly, this woman hails from the land of Shimamura!"

"Sounds like a nice place. I should move there."

I pinched the fabric of my culottes and stared down at them. What part of this outfit gave her Shimamura Co. vibes? I hardly ever bought clothes there, but that didn't matter, apparently. *Hino thinks she can treat me like their poster child, just because we have the same name.*

So, there I was, at the fishing hole with Hino bright and early Sunday morning. We originally made plans to fish on Saturday, but then it rained, so we postponed it. Fortunately, I didn't have plans today either, so it worked out.

I hadn't brought any fishing gear, but as it turned out, Hino dressed fairly normally. I expected her to show up wearing one of those vests with all the pockets on the front, but nope—the most eye-catching thing she wore was an oversized straw hat. Smirking, she fiddled with the brim.

"Call me Sanpei the Fisher Girl."

"Who?"

"You haven't heard of *Sanpei*? Good grief. Kids these days," she sighed. Two seconds later, her sunny smile returned in a flash of inspiration. "She just don't know what Hi-knows! Get it?"

"Oh my god, shut up."

And so, the Punmaster led me out behind the local elementary school. I'd gone to a different elementary, so I had no idea that there was a fishing hole out here.

Next to the pond was a little store that sold school uniforms and whatnot. We stood beside it in the shade it afforded. Cirrocumulus clouds peppered the autumn sky, and the temperature was relatively mild, but the sun's rays still retained the strength of summer. I was right to bring a parasol.

"Where's Nagafuji? I know she was busy with club stuff on Saturday, but what about today?"

"I invited her, but she said she hates fish. This is the *fifth* time she's shot me down!" Hino exclaimed gleefully, holding up her hand in a "five" gesture.

That made sense; Nagafuji was more of a "burgers and curry" kind of gal. Mild curry only, though. Absently, I wondered about Adachi's preferences, thinking back to her clear skin and the way she chugged her mineral water.

"Now, I humbly present you with this 300-yen fishing rod I bought from a priest at the flea market."

"Gee, I'm so...*honored*. Thanks," I replied as I accepted the rod. It was thin and had a simple design—as though someone had just taken a tree branch they found on the ground and painted it black. I probably wouldn't have known that it was a fishing rod if no one had told me outright. Hino's rod, meanwhile, was shorter and made of bamboo.

"For the record, this one is a rental. 500 yen per day."

"You rented it? When? From where?"

"It's a mystery."

Apparently, that was all she had to say about it. She reached into her bag and fumbled around as though she were looking for something.

"By the way, Shimamura-chan..."

"Yeah?"

"You're not gonna start chickening out about having to bait your hook, are you?"

She pulled out a small tackle box and opened the lid to reveal that the box was crammed full of lively little worms, wriggling and squirming and—

I leapt back as the blood drained from my face. She grabbed one between her thumb and index finger and shot me a concerned smile.

"You can't handle a few creepy-crawlies?"

"No way. *Noooo way.*" I held my hands up defensively. Frankly, it was a miracle I didn't scream.

"Fine, fine, if you insist..."

She closed the worm box and took out a different one. I braced myself for some other variety of gross, but when she opened the box, all it held was some sort of yellow putty. *Fish eat this?*

"I made some paste bait for us yesterday. You can have some."

"Paste...? I have no idea what I'm looking at, but thanks." *I'd take literally anything over having to touch a worm.* "What's it made of?"

"Wheat flour, water, eggs...plus a bit of my special sauce. Some people use ground-up salmon roe."

"*Salmon roe?* What a waste," I mused. *I'd sooner eat it myself.*

"I also brought you a big ol' bucket, so feel free to hook as many as you can catch! Aren't you excited?!" she shouted, shooting me a thumbs-up as she handed me the metal bucket. *Is that supposed to be sarcasm?*

After we baited our hooks, we positioned ourselves on

one of the bamboo platforms around the pond, then cast our lines. I say "pond," but really, this so-called fishing hole was more of a glorified puddle. *Seriously, I've seen kiddie pools bigger than this.* The water was murky, its depths unknown.

"I feel like it'd be faster to wade in and grab the fish with our bare hands," I joked, extending my leg as though I was going to dip my toe in.

"You'll come out covered in leeches, but by all means, knock yourself out."

I retracted my leg at the speed of light. *On second thought, I think I'll stick to the slow method.* For a moment, I stared out at the water's surface. I was already bored of holding the parasol, so I started spinning it.

Five or so minutes went by.

"So, what's Adachi like?" Hino asked out of nowhere.

I cocked my head in confusion. *Talk about random.* "Uh, I don't know... Normal?"

"That's not much of an answer, Shima-moo."

Ugh, don't give me a weird nickname. Well, anything's better than Shimamura, I guess. "Why do you want to know about her?"

"Just curious, that's all. It's not every day you get to meet a capital-D delinquent!" Hino gave a goofy little laugh.

Adachi didn't strike me as a "capital-D" delinquent, though. All she really did was cut class, albeit to an extreme degree. Outside of that, she wasn't much different from any other girl. She didn't do anything gossip-worthy. *Actually, she's even more scared of creepy-crawlies than I am.*

"C'mon. You know her better than anyone else, right?" Hino prompted.

"I wouldn't say that." *Then again, now that I think about it, Adachi did say I'm her only friend.* "Actually, maybe so."

"Make up your mind, would you?! Look...I just want to get to know your other friends, that's all."

"Right."

"And if you like her, then she must be pretty cool."

"Right..."

I liked Hino's unwavering optimism, I really did, but I just wasn't sure Adachi would want to make friends with her. Adachi didn't strike me as the type to enjoy having a bunch of friends; I couldn't picture her opening up like that. Yet, for some reason, she seemed to think *I* was the antisocial one. *Me, of all people. Yeah, right.*

Crawly critters aside, I enjoyed lots of things. Like staring at the sky, or eating sweets. I liked Rilakkuma and Mickey Mouse, too. *Wait... None of those are people... Okay, forget those.*

74

"Well? What's she like?"

"Mmm...I'm not sure where to start. Honestly, I don't really know that much about her myself."

For example, I had no idea how Adachi spent her Sundays. I decided to stick to inoffensive subjects like her neighborhood and favorite foods.

"She really likes to drink water. Especially mineral water. She doesn't seem to care what brand."

Not that there were a lot of brands to choose from. The school vending machines only stocked Crystal Geyser, so that's what she drank.

"I see. So, she's a Namekian."

"Maybe. I haven't seen her regrow any arms, though. Oh, and she lives over that way."

"Interesting." Hino nodded pensively.

In the interest of protecting Adachi's privacy, I was making an active effort to keep things vague—so vague, in fact, that I wasn't sure they were all that useful. If Hino still found them interesting, however, then maybe I didn't need to worry after all. *Meh, Hino probably just wants to win Adachi over by buying treats for her. Who knows if it'll work, though?*

Come to think of it, the whole reason had Hino invited me out here in the first place was to meet some astronaut LARPer. The fishing part was just supposed to be a side perk. So, where was my promised weirdo? There were a few other people at the fishing hole, but they all looked like ordinary dudes in their forties or fifties. Did the spaceman have other business today? Not that I especially wanted to meet them. I was fine spending a peaceful day standing around.

But, the very next moment, a voice directly behind me asked, "Anything biting?"

I was so startled, I almost dropped my fishing pole. Then I turned around and jumped out of my skin *again*. This time, I nearly fell backward into the pond.

Standing there was a person wearing a bright-white space suit. Needless to say, they stuck out like a sore thumb.

"Oh, hey, there you are!" Hino greeted the astronaut. "Glad you could make it today. Otherwise, I would've dragged Shimamura out here for nothing!"

So, this is the weirdo Hino was talking about. That's right—I think she mentioned that they wore a space suit. I wasn't really paying attention then.

"Krrrssshhh...krrrssshhh..." The astronaut made weird breathing sounds through their helmet.

"Wow, you weren't kidding," I said. "They're weird, all right."

Light glinted off the space suit's opaque visor, blinding me. The whole suit was rather simple in design, not unlike my fishing pole. Although the helmet succeeded in con-cealing the astronaut's face, it was obvious from their voice that they were female. Judging from her height, she was probably a grade schooler... But, if so, I was getting a little concerned about where she was headed in life. If she was an adult, there was no hope left for her.

"Who might this be?"

Everything from the neck up pivoted from me to Hino and back. On first glance, the total lack of exposed skin gave me the impression that the suit was bulky and restrictive, but the astronaut's movements were surpris-ingly fluid. Maybe her space suit wasn't as heavy as a real one.

"This is *the* Shimamura."

"What's *that* supposed to mean...?"

Ignoring my indignant question, Astronaut Girl stared up at me curiously. "Aha... We meet at last."

I didn't want to have to call her "Astronaut Girl" for the rest of time, so I decided to put myself out there and ask for her name directly.

"So, uhhh...what's your name?"

It was a fairly mundane question, and yet her visor seemed to glint smugly in the sunlight.

"Heh heh heh! Unlike my foolish compatriot, I made sure to think of a name in advance!"

For some reason, she sounded very proud of this.

She put her hands on her hips and declared, "You may call me Chikama Yashiro! Krrrssshhh...krrrssshhh..."

Chikama Yashiro. What a weird name. Not that it was any weirder than her breathing noises, mind you. She had a fishing pole slung over her shoulder, so evidently she was here to fish, just like we were. The middle-aged fishermen didn't seem surprised to see her, either. *Why would an astronaut have fishing gear, anyway?*

Needless to say, it was pretty surreal.

"I've come to Planet Earth in search of my compatriot."

"Your what now?" *Oh, I get it. Her friend, in other words. Wait, did she just say "Planet Earth"?*

"My compatriot came to this planet on a mission and hasn't returned. Thus, I was dispatched as the search party, but it appears I've landed in the wrong spot. Krrrssshhh... krrrssshhh..."

The longer her sentences, the heavier her breathing. *You know, you wouldn't have such a hard time getting oxygen if you just took the helmet off. Is your buddy wearing the same outfit? That should make them easy to spot, at least.*

Surrounded by this oppressive awkwardness, I really wasn't sure how to respond. Then Hino clapped me on the shoulder. "Alrighty then! Have fun communicating with the unknown!"

"What?"

"Ooh, I'm getting a reading on my fish-dar! Signs of life *waaaay* over there!"

Hino wandered away, babbling to herself. I was half-tempted to grab Chikama Yashiro by the scruff of the neck and shout, "YOU FORGOT YOUR WEIRDO!" But then I realized the real reason Hino had brought me here: she wanted me to babysit this kid. *I* was the bait.

Meanwhile, for some reason, Chikama Yashiro was setting up camp next to me. Her worms were so wriggly, she'd probably found them on the ground right there. And, although she wore gloves as part of her costume, I was still impressed by how comfortable she was spearing the worms with her hook.

"So, you're Shimamura-san, eh?"

"Huh? Oh, uh, yeah. I guess Hino told you about me?"

I hoped to find out what exactly Hino said to her, but somehow doubted I'd get a straight answer.

"I'm told the natives visit you frequently. You must be popular."

"That's the other Shimamura, not me," I corrected her as I cast my line. I did *not* want her mistaking me for Shimamura Co.

"No need to be modest. Oh, but just so we're clear, I am not one of the natives. I came here from the future."

"And I came here from the past. Nice to meet you."

Whatever, I'm gonna roll with it. She's not just weird, she's nuttier than a fruitcake. And there's more than one of them? I'm starting to think Planet Earth is in trouble.

"You appear to be an ordinary Earthling."

"Yep."

"Krrrssshhh...krrrssshhh..."

"You can take your helmet off, you know."

But this self-proclaimed "time traveler" simply shook her head. "My face isn't ready yet. It needs more time."

"What is this, *Anpanman*?"

I was already tired of the girl. With every passing minute, I envied Hino more and more. Meanwhile, she was on the opposite bank, deftly hauling up one fish after another. She spotted me looking at her and smirked down her nose at me. *God, I want to punch you.*

Still, I had to hand it to her: she had turned her lame excuse into the truth through sheer talent. Somehow, she saw through these murky depths to the treasure lurking within. No amateur could manage that.

I glanced out of the corner of my eye at the weirdo next to me to see how she was doing. She was enjoying a peaceful moment, waiting for the fish to bite. *Wait, what?*

"Don't you need to go look for your friend—I mean, compatriot?" I asked.

"I have grown hungry," she replied matter-of-factly.

Something about it struck me as poetic. Pretty delusional of me, I know.

"Now that I have confirmed my compatriot's relative safety, I feel comfortable taking a moment to relax."

"Oh. So, you got in touch with them?" I asked casually.

There was a long pause.

"Well... Something to that effect."

What are you trying to imply? And for that matter—

"If you've already made contact with them, can't you just meet up whenever you want?"

"There are...extenuating circumstances," she replied quickly, then got really quiet, as though she was trying to be mysterious. Personally, I appreciated the silence, but her sudden change of attitude made me curious. That said, I strongly doubted that any further questions I asked would lead to answers that made sense. One look at the space suit, and that much was obvious.

As for my fishing line, it wasn't even twitching. *This is boring.*

"Seems like nothing's biting, huh?"

"Yes, that's the perfect mindset."

"What?"

"When nothing's biting, when it's not going very well, that means there is infinite potential for change,"

Chikama Yashiro explained. She hauled up her line, expertly cutting through the water, only to reveal a barren hook. Then she happily cast the line back into the pond. *Were you just practicing or what?*

Meanwhile, Ms. Straw Hat on the other bank was having the time of her life, shouting "FISH!" with every catch.

"From there, all that's left is to cast your line and hope for a better future," the astronaut continued optimistically, gazing out at her line as her stomach rumbled. If I ignored all the nutjob comments she made earlier, that almost sounded like good advice that could apply in a lot of cases.

For example, the stuffy gym loft.

Maybe I just have to put myself out there.

"And that's the gist of what happened," I finished, after recounting Sunday's events to Adachi at lunch on Monday.

"Huh," she replied, sounding less than interested. Her voice was as dry as a pile of autumn leaves.

"Oh, I'm sorry, was I *boring* you?"

For the record, Chikama Yashiro ended up catching five, maybe six fish. *I wonder if she actually ate them.*

"No, you weren't boring me. Don't be so passive-aggressive."

"You're right. Sorry."

Adachi and I were hanging out in the gym loft, as usual. No sign of Hino or Nagafuji, and I got the sense that Adachi was happy about that. For me, it was a lot easier not having to play mediator between her and the others. My friendship with Adachi was just too different from the one I shared with them.

Was it my fault, or was it Adachi's fault?

I decided not to think about it.

I sat with my back against the wall and my legs splayed out; she lay on the floor, using my thigh as a pillow. Supposedly things had gotten hectic at her part-time job last night, so she was exhausted. That surprised me somewhat, because I didn't know she had a part-time job at all. *Now I know what she gets up to on her days off.*

"Where do you work, anyway?"

"Not telling," she shot back, rolling onto her side. Her cheek felt nice and cool against my skin.

"Aww, why not?"

"Because I know you'll come see me."

"You're right. I totally would."

"Well, I don't *want* you to. It's too embarrassing."

She pushed her face against my leg, and her silky hair fell like a curtain, concealing most of her expression. I grabbed a lock of hair and ran it through my fingers; it slipped away so fast, it practically evaporated.

"Aww, c'mon! There's nothing to be ashamed of! If anything, you should be proud to have a job!" I insisted, patronizingly stroking her hair as a joke. I expected her to slap my hand away, but...she didn't. Maybe she was just too tired to fight it.

Her jacket hung from the ping-pong table, where she'd thrown it, and her shoes lay scattered on the floor. *Absolutely no sense of decorum, this one.*

She rolled over to face me, her cheek brushing my skirt. I squirmed slightly as gravity pulled her hair down onto my leg, tickling me. Meanwhile, Adachi stared blankly at my stomach area, blinking hard, as though she was trying to will away drowsiness. Her nose twitched slightly, and she smiled.

"I think I like facing this way the best."

"Yeah?" Personally, I figured the limited field of vision would feel claustrophobic.

Adachi leaned closer, her nose in the air. "Yeah... This way I can smell your scent."

"Wait, what? Do I stink or something?" That was news to me. I felt my self-esteem getting ready to plummet.

"That's not what I mean... Fine, I won't do it, then."

What? Why is she pouting all of a sudden?

"Shimamura, you have no class."

"No class? Hmm. No one's ever said *that* to me, either."

"Classiness" was a concept I rarely encountered in my day-to-day life. Out in the sticks, we were about as uncultured as you could get.

Adachi and I were twenty minutes into lunch break, and we still hadn't eaten. Even if I wanted to go grab food, Adachi was using me as a pillow, so I couldn't move. After all, she hardly ever showed affection like this; it'd be cruel to shove her off, onto the floor.

I looked back at the clock, even though I'd only just checked it. Somehow, I dreaded every tick of the second hand. Soon lunch would end, cleanup would begin...and then what?

"Hey, Adachi?"

"Hmm?" she responded softly, without looking up.

"Wanna go to class with me after lunch?" I asked, stroking her hair.

She raised her head, then pushed herself up off the floor. Toying with her hair, she peered into my eyes. "Where'd that come from?"

"Well, you need to attend class a certain number of

days, or else... I mean, wouldn't it be more fun to pass our first year and be second-years together?"

There was no telling whether we'd end up in the same class again, but passing together would at least be less awkward than Adachi getting held back. I mean, the idea of her being junior to me was kind of funny to think about, but when I imagined myself as her senpai, it didn't feel right.

Then again, I hadn't exactly kept track of her attendance, so it was possible she'd already exceeded the maximum permissible absences. Still, I'd meant to suggest this idea for a while.

First I started skipping class, then I met Adachi, then I started asking her to go to class with me. Something about that felt distinctly out of order, or maybe inconsistent. But I couldn't just kick back and enjoy the status quo. Not while the threat of flunking loomed on the horizon.

I attended this school on my family's dime, not my own. If I got held back, they'd probably throw me out on the street. They were typically fairly hands-off, which is why they expected me to behave responsibly. Failure to do so would result in harsh consequences.

"Uhh...well..."

Scratching her cheek, Adachi looked around, surveying the loft. Once she'd had her fill, she collapsed back onto my leg. Apparently, she liked it there.

"Sure... I guess it can't hurt every now and then," she conceded.

Of course, that wasn't very convincing coming from the girl sprawled out in lounge mode on the floor. But at least she hadn't said no. I knew she generally acted on a whim, and since she specified "every now and then," chances were high that she'd go right back to skipping class the next day. Nevertheless, something about this felt reassuring, almost like a cool breeze had blown through the stuffy loft.

"In that case, we should go somewhere after class," Adachi suggested, raising her head. She sounded enthusiastic, which was a good sign. "Got any plans with anyone?"

"Nope, not today. To be honest, I almost never have plans."

"Gotcha." She rested her head back onto my thigh... in relief? Truth be told, my whole leg was starting to go numb, but whatever.

The idea of going somewhere with Adachi was actually kind of a novelty. After all, she was usually already gone by the time the final bell rang.

"Okay then, how about we stop by the place where you work?"

"I told you, I don't want you to visit!"

She turned her back to me, pouting. It reminded me of a little kid who didn't want their mom to visit them at school. I understood the feeling, though; if it were me, I'd probably be just as opposed. High school was basically its own separate society, and it was always weird to see elements leak out into the "real" world. I could imagine why some people would want to live at school full-time.

But I digress.

I wanted a better future, so I cast my line in Adachi's direction. Not that I was actually taking cues from that time-traveling astronaut or anything.

"Looks like I landed a big one," I murmured. But the way Adachi had settled on my lap reminded me less of a fish and more of a puppy.

Yep, she definitely likes it there.

When we entered the classroom, we attracted a bit of attention—probably because Adachi had actually shown up for class, plus I was with her. We were both seen as bad kids, after all.

Biting back a yawn, Adachi looked around the classroom. *Did she forget where she's supposed to sit?* Her desk was by the door, right at the very front. As for me, I sat over by the windows, three desks down. Because our assigned seats were so far apart, we ended up going our separate ways soon after walking in.

Once I sat down, I started taking out materials for our next class. Then it hit me. *Did Adachi bring her textbook?* Curious, I glanced over...and saw her desk stacked high with every single textbook for every single class. Apparently, she'd left them all in the classroom.

Once she found the right one, she put the others back, then leaned her elbow on her desk with her face in her palm. She evidently didn't feel like getting out a pencil or anything else. She glanced over at the windows—probably at me. It was so sudden that I didn't look away in time.

She seemed surprised to find me peering at her, but it was too late to look away. So, instead, we exchanged silent "What?" looks a dozen or so times. I was admittedly the one who started it, so logically, it was up to me to answer the question...but how? I couldn't exactly shout across the classroom at her.

Instead, I pointed to her textbook. Maybe that way she would understand why I was looking at her. She lowered her gaze and stared at the book for a moment.

Meanwhile, I admired the symmetrical slope of her face in profile.

She looked back at me and mouthed something I couldn't quite catch, so she repeated it. *Did you forget your textbook?*

Much as I wanted to take offense at that, I couldn't exactly pretend that I was an honor student. To Adachi and everyone else, there was no notable difference between us. That was my fault, 100 percent.

The teacher walked in. He seemed surprised to see both me and Adachi at our desks; he shot us each a curious glance, but otherwise said nothing as he walked to the lectern and stood behind it.

Class started, and I wondered just how long it had been since Adachi and I last shared a classroom. Her attendance had been a bit better during first semester, but naturally I hadn't paid attention to her then. Now, however, I was extremely, weirdly conscious of her. Terrified that she might catch me looking again, I focused all my energy into not glancing in her direction. Instead, I simply followed along with whatever the teacher wrote on the chalkboard.

As my eyes and hand moved on autopilot, my brain was left to twiddle its thumbs. In my boredom, I found myself wondering why I couldn't get a read on the emotional distance between myself and Adachi. Was it because one of us was unstable?

That was all that occupied my thoughts as I copied down my notes like a robot.

"How'd it feel to be back in class after so long?"

"History class was great, but math... I have no idea how to do anything anymore."

"Ha ha ha... Oh, you..."

I didn't know how to do anything in math either, and I went to class *way* more often than she did. *Maybe I'm just a more right-brained person. Yeah, that's it.*

After school, as per our agreement, Adachi and I left together. Once again, her bookbag was practically empty.

"Everybody was looking at you today, huh, Shimamura?" she commented, glancing back down the hallway at the classroom door. I hadn't noticed.

"Nah. They were probably looking at *you*."

"Nope. It was you," she insisted firmly.

How does she know that for a fact? I don't get it.

"Probably because you're so beautiful," she continued casually. I was caught so completely off-guard that I nearly walked straight into the wall ahead of me. I jumped back in the nick of time and almost lost my balance.

"Having fun over there?" Adachi asked dryly, one foot on the stairs. *Don't you laugh at me! This is YOUR fault!*

"I've just...never been called beautiful before, that's all." My relatives *had* called me "pretty" in the past, but they were only being nice.

"Really? Not even by your boyfriend?"

"I've never had one."

"Huh," Adachi replied, as though she was unsure how to react to that information. She looked up, her expression stoic. "I guess they're all blind idiots, then."

Right back at you, I wanted to say, but I didn't want to shoot down her compliment.

At the bottom of the staircase, we arrived at the shoe lockers. "So, where do you want to go?" I asked, changing the subject.

"We didn't eat lunch today, so I'm kinda hungry," Adachi answered as she changed into her outdoor shoes.

"Okay then, wanna grab a bite somewhere?"

She glanced around pensively, rubbing her stomach. "I could go for something simple, like donuts."

"Donuts, huh? Okay then, let's go. The closest place is over by the train station."

We left the school building and started walking. Although the station square was a bit far from here, I didn't mind.

But when we reached the school gates, and Adachi was still standing next to me, I couldn't help but ask, "Uh, what about your bike?"

"I didn't take it to school today. Had to get it repaired." She acted as if that was no big deal, but I knew the walk from her house was pretty lengthy.

"Whoa... I'm kinda impressed that you'd bother walking all this way to school. Y'know, since you're a delinquent and all. Good for you!" I joked.

But she didn't even crack a smile. Instead, she shrank down and mumbled, "Well... I thought maybe you'd be here."

She was practically implying that I was the entire reason she bothered to show up. Embarrassed, I fumbled for a response. "Y-yeah."

Unfortunately, my awkwardness seemed to make Adachi feel awkward, too; she turned a bit red in the face. Or maybe I was just seeing things. *What is this weird tension between us?*

My whole body grew uncomfortably stiff, like a piece of beef jerky, as we walked to the station in uneasy silence. I wasn't even that tired, yet my legs felt like lead. Every now and then, I felt a gaze. When I turned to look, sure enough, our eyes would meet. Then, like clockwork, we'd both immediately look away.

What is this? What is happening right now?

We carried that bizarre tension all the way to the station—a shabby, two-story building frequented by students and adults alike. Once we'd stepped inside, we walked straight into the Mister Donut to the left of the entrance. The shop was crammed full of train commuters both young and old, so there was nowhere for us to sit. Worse still, there was a long line at the register.

"Looks like everybody wants donuts today," I mused, glancing around.

That finally got a smile out of Adachi. "I love the way it smells in here. Nice and sugary." She took a big sniff of the cloying fragrance that permeated the store—so thick, it was practically a meal all on its own.

"Reminds me of ants on honey."

At that, Adachi grimaced. "Gross. I do *not* like that analogy."

Right. I forgot how much she hates bugs. At least now we're actually talking to each other, though.

"Which one are you gonna get?" she asked, enthusiasm steadily returning to her voice and body language. Seriously, we had both been total stone statues on the way to the train station, so it was refreshing to see her acting like a human again...not to mention a major relief.

"I always have a hard time choosing, but I'll probably get an Angel French. Plus two extras to take home to my little sister."

Whenever I approached the counter, I was prone to getting distracted by all the appetizing options, but ultimately I always fell back on the Angel French donut. My mom bought them for me as a treat when I was little, so at this point they were probably imprinted in my brain as a comfort food or something.

"You too, huh?" Adachi struck a pensive pose. Was she going to get the same donut?

"What's wrong?" I asked.

"Well, I don't want to order the same thing."

"Why not? What's the harm?"

"Mmmm...I'll just get this one." She took a Honey Dip donut from the lower rack as she spoke. *I guess she doesn't want to seem like a copycat.* As we waited in line, carrying our chosen donuts on a tray, she asked me, "Are you going to class again tomorrow?"

"Yeah, probably. Wouldn't want them to think I've given up entirely, you know."

"Gotcha."

That wasn't to suggest that I was never going back to the loft, or anything like that; Adachi and I would have plenty more opportunities to hang out.

Smirking at her curt response, I peered into her eyes. "Care to *join* me, Adachi-san?" I asked her in my best theatrical voice.

For a moment she seemed caught off-guard, but then she laughed. "Sure, maybe just for a few more days."

Despite her surprise, she didn't put up much resistance to the proposal. She was like me; she skipped school for no deeper reason than because she felt like it. And now she simply felt like attending class for a change.

After a loooong wait, we paid for our food and left. Once we were outside, we found a free spot near the escalators and decided to eat our donuts leaning against the wall. Adachi took out my Angel French, opened the wrapper, curled a napkin underneath, and handed it to me.

"Thanks." I took the donut and immediately sank my teeth into the chocolate dip. "Mmm, sugar."

I hadn't eaten anything since breakfast that morning. The donut overloaded my taste buds with an intensity only matched by sour candy—though the flavor was completely different, of course. It was *so* good. The blissful sweetness danced across my tongue and teeth.

Meanwhile, Adachi ate her donut by pulling it apart one piece at a time. While her method certainly *looked* more elegant, it was an easy way to get your fingers sticky, which is why I preferred to bite the donut directly. *Then again, my method usually ends with me getting sugar all over my face, so I guess it evens out.*

"That reminds me—Hino asked about you yesterday," I told her as we ate. She fell still and looked away.

"Which one is Hino again? The short one?"

"Yeah, the shorter one. She said she wants to get to know you."

"Gotcha."

"Yeah... I figured you wouldn't be interested," I muttered under my breath. Evidently, Hino had her work cut out for her. *But, then, how did I make friends with Adachi so easily?* I wasn't sure what it was about me specifically that set me apart.

"So, you said you have a little sister?"

I debated whether to let Adachi change the subject, then ultimately decided to go along with it. "Yeah, I do."

"How old?"

"She's in fourth grade. But, to me, she's just a baby."

According to my mom, my sister acted a lot different when she wasn't at home. She was apparently a model student at school—soft-spoken and mature. That was nothing like the way she acted at our house, where she often unleashed her "ultimate attacks" on me mercilessly. The stark contrast actually reminded me of Adachi, in a way.

"A mini-Shimamura, huh...? I bet she's cute."

"She is...when she's not kicking me or being a brat," I answered absently.

"Lucky," Adachi murmured, smiling softly. Maybe she'd always wanted a sibling or something. *I guess that means she's an only child.*

She tore off another piece of her donut and offered it to me. "Want some?"

"Oh, um...sure."

I leaned forward and bit the donut piece right out from between her fingers. The honey glaze's sweetness spread across my tongue, making my teeth ache. It was even more sugary than my Angel French's cream filling.

"You can have some of mine, too," I said, offering her my half-eaten donut. She stared at it, unmoving. *What's the problem?* I wondered, looking down at the donut with her. Then I realized. "Ohhh, I get it." I took another small bite so that the cream filling was clearly visible, then offered her the donut again. "This is what you wanted, right?"

"Okay then...since you're offering," she replied vaguely.

She took a bite, chewed, and swallowed. It was strikingly elegant for a girl who never bothered to wear her uniform properly, and I wondered if perhaps Adachi's parents were strict with her at home.

"Where do you want to go after we're done?" I asked her, wiping the sugar from the corners of my mouth.

The train station had plenty of restaurants where businessmen could get drunk after a hard day at the office. However, not many places targeted a teenage demographic. In addition to the Mister Donut, the first floor had a grocery store, a bakery, and a MOS Burger—nothing but food, food, and more food. There was also a Matsumotokiyoshi, but I didn't really feel the need to wander through a drugstore.

"Not a lot of places to shop around here, huh?" Adachi commented.

"I know, right? This place is nothing like Nagoya."

"Yeah, but Nagoya's always so crowded. I think I like it better here," she laughed. I could agree with the first half of that, at least. I popped the rest of my donut into my mouth and zoned out while I waited for Adachi to finish hers.

In elementary school, my teachers always wrote "inattentive; lacks focus" on my report cards. To be honest, they weren't wrong. My mind *loved* to wander;

whenever there was a quiet period, I always ended up lost in thought. I lived for the moment when a daydream took root, whisking me away from the five senses chaining me to reality. In that regard, maybe I preferred being alone. After all, spacing out while in another person's company was generally frowned upon.

"Okay, I'm done," Adachi announced, wiping her hands with a napkin. At times like these, I envied her mostly-empty bookbag.

"All right then, uh...let's go."

We didn't have a set destination in mind, but we set off walking nonetheless. Our legs moved automatically, carrying us to the exit.

If I'd come to the train station alone, I would have wandered around absently, then gone home when my feet started to hurt. But today I had Adachi with me, and that meant I had to consider her needs, in case she had a bad time. The longer I was obligated to spend time thinking about that, the more it started to feel like *work*. Hanging out with people was always a little miserable for me because of that.

Being considerate, dealing with problems, repairing or ending friendships... So much emotional labor. Yet I knew the key to happiness hid somewhere underneath all that misery, like a child's toy lying forgotten in the backyard.

I wanted to believe that meeting Adachi had changed my future for the better.

As we walked outside the station, I felt a sudden squeeze. I couldn't speak—I was too shocked. Instead, I stopped short and turned to look.

Adachi had grabbed me by the hand. Her gaze flitted around timidly, as though she was trying to gauge my reaction.

Now, if that had happened because I'd zoned out to the point that I was about to walk into traffic, it would've made sense. But that wasn't the case.

"Oh, uh, I can let go if it bothers you. Just let me know," Adachi blurted out.

Her nervous energy made *me* nervous, too. I looked from the station building to the border fence to the "Under Construction" sign hanging from the overpass.

"It doesn't really bother me. I just wasn't expecting it," I explained.

Seriously, for a minute there I'd thought it was a purse-snatcher or a really aggressive guy trying to hit on me or something. I was relieved, if anything, to find that it wasn't the work of a stranger. But, to be honest, I was resistant to the idea of holding hands with Adachi, regardless of her reasons. It kinda felt like we were flaunting our friendship for all the world to see, and that made me uncomfortable.

Yet, despite that, I was somehow totally fine with her lying on my lap earlier.

"Should I let go?"

"No, it's fine. Come on."

I couldn't bear to wrest my hand away; I wasn't capable of being that rude to another person. Instead, I gripped her hand back and started walking again, consciously keeping my head held high and my posture perfectly straight. If I let my guard down for even a second, I felt as though I might slouch my shoulders in shame.

It caught me by surprise, but now that I was thinking rationally, holding hands was hardly that unusual. Granted, I hadn't seen any girls at our school do it, but sometimes I glimpsed women walking arm in arm downtown. At those times, I dismissed it as something that would never happen to me—until now. It felt weird to be on the other side for a change.

Last time I held hands with someone was...Sports Day, back in grade school. Wow, that was a pretty long time ago.

Adachi's hand was soft and squishy, if a bit fidgety.

"I didn't know you were such a needy little baby," I mused.

"I'm not...*needy*," she replied, though I could hear uncertainty in her voice.

As we headed down the road, she gave my hand a couple tiny squeezes. The way she seemed to beg for my affection was driving me crazy.

"I had no idea," I repeated absently, proving how surprised I was. If someone had told me back when Adachi and I were eating donuts that this would happen, I probably wouldn't have believed them.

"Is it weird? Because, to me, this is...pretty normal."

Obviously you *think it's normal, or else you wouldn't have initiated it. The problem is that I don't understand* why *you did it.*

As we walked, her hand was all I could think about. Did she do this with everyone? Maybe I just didn't know about it because I hadn't walked anywhere with her until today. Some people needed a little physical reassurance to combat anxiety and things like that; maybe she was one of those people. She probably wasn't a closet lesbian or anything like that...probably.

I couldn't bear to look at her, so I stared straight ahead.

She probably wasn't gay for me...but what if she was? What if she asked me out? What would I do then?

"Where are we going, Shimamura?"

"Huh? Oh, I haven't really decided. Any suggestions?"

"Wherever you wanna go is fine with me."

That was the least helpful answer she could have given me. When two passive people needed to make a choice, it always turned into a game of hot potato. But, in my view, Adachi was *clearly* more responsible than I was. So, really, it was *her* decision to make. As it stood, we were no better than two lost children wandering around without our parents. Like Hansel and Gretel or something.

I felt Adachi's fingers twitching...no, *pulsing*. And as I concentrated on that tiny pulse, I twitched my fingers in kind. In response, she shifted slightly, and the pulse disappeared. In a way, it reminded me of fishing—each side carefully testing the waters, each side searching for something.

So, what was Adachi searching for within me?

There were admittedly a lot of things we had yet to talk about, but I was pretty much an open book.

By this point, I couldn't focus on anything else, not even the scenery around us. I needed to snap myself out of it, fast. It felt as though this information overload would give me brain freeze and make me scream my head off like a lunatic otherwise.

Where should we go? Shopping? Noooo, no, no. No way.

Now that I've got her caught on my hook...should I go ahead and reel her in all the way to my house?

Just before I could suggest it to her, I heard a familiar grating...chirp?...right behind us.

"Krrrssshhh…krrrssshhh…"

"Whoa!"

Together, Adachi and I spun around. Sure enough, there stood the astronaut from yesterday. At least, I was pretty sure it was the same person, since they were the exact same height.

Our town was kind of small, but for someone on foot, it was still a fairly big place. Yet, somehow, I'd managed to encounter this girl two days in a row.

The clear sky glinted off her visor, and when her helmet wobbled, a galaxy of blue sparkles lit up like stars.

"Hello there," she greeted us, bowing politely.

"Uhhh…hey," I replied, reflexively bowing back.

"Saw you passing by, so I thought I'd say hi. Krrrssshhh…krrrssshhh…"

"Is…is that what the 'krrrsshhh' sound is supposed to signify?"

I felt the conversation giving me an ulcer. Then I realized that Adachi was no longer holding my hand, though I couldn't remember when she'd let go. She stood a short distance away from me, cradling her hand protectively. *Her nose looks a bit red—is she blushing? She didn't seem that embarrassed walking down the street, though… I don't get it.*

"So, you walk around town in that getup, do you?" I asked.

"It is all I have to wear."

She doesn't have any other clothes?

The longer I talked to Chikama Yashiro, the more I felt the world around us silently judging me. *Oh well.* Truth be told, this had actually helped me break out of the self-consciousness I felt holding hands with Adachi.

I reached out for the girl's helmet, and she hastily shuffled backward. I wiggled my fingers at her teasingly for a moment, and when I stopped, she quietly shuffled forward again. The more she resisted, the more I wanted to snatch the helmet off her head.

Then Chikama Yashiro (you know what, let's just call her Yashiro for short) brought her face—er, helmet—close to my fingers.

"I smell something wonderful and sweet emanating from your fingertips."

Like ants to honey, indeed. Better Yashiro than an actual bug, though. She pressed her visor against my hand, as if to imply that she was sniffing it, though I couldn't tell one way or the other. In fact, it was impressive that she managed to smell *anything* through that giant, heavy helmet. *What if she's secretly a talking dog?*

I could see the reflection of my face in her visor. Shifting my perspective, I spotted Adachi's reflection, too. Her expression was decidedly unamused.

"What is this lovely smell? I rather like it."

"Donuts, probably. We just ate some."

"Donuts?" Yashiro tilted her head. Then her helmet turned toward the to-go bag in my hand. I instinctively hid the bag behind my back, and a split-second later, Yashiro's gloved hands closed on the empty air where it once hung.

"What do you think you're doing? And how did I know you would do it?"

"I've detected donuts on my radar."

"Yes, there are donuts in here, but they're not for you. This isn't the fishing hole."

For that matter, I'm pretty sure the fishing hole charges money to fish there. Did Yashiro even pay?

"Give me a...donut?...and I shall tell you one of the secrets of the universe," she declared, holding her index finger aloft.

"Wow, for free? Golly," I replied dryly.

Why should I have to give you a donut? I thought to myself. Then I realized: *If she eats something, then that means she'll have to take her helmet off. And if I'm here, THAT means I'll get to see her face!* I'd been dying to know what she looked like since yesterday, so to me, that was quite the enticing bait.

"Fine, you can have one. But just *one*."

"Wow!" The way she lifelessly raised her arms into the air, I couldn't tell if she was being sincere or sarcastic.

Meh, my sister doesn't really need more than one. Besides, if I spoil her too much, she won't want to eat dinner, and Mom will get pissed at me.

After a brief internal debate, I ultimately decided to hand over the Custard Cream.

"So, this is a donut...oh ho...oh hooOOoooh..."

Is she trying to sound impressed? To me, she sounds like an owl.

Instead of removing her helmet like I'd hoped, Yashiro raised her visor a tiny fraction and wedged the donut in like a letter through a mail slot. The loud, wet chewing sounds that followed were some of the grossest noises I'd ever heard. *How does she manage to inspire repulsion AND disappointment at the same time?*

"This is heavenly! It's so sugary sweet!"

In stark contrast to me and Adachi, Yashiro was on cloud nine, her helmet wobbling to and fro.

"Normally I'd say it's weird that you've never had a donut before, but...in your case, that's hardly the weirdest thing about you." Still, it was nice to see her so overjoyed.

"Got anything sweeter?"

I felt her gaze bore into me through her visor. Annoyed, I put my hand on my hip.

"You want more? Go buy your own."

"I don't have any money!"

And you're proud of that why, exactly? "How can you possibly survive without—"

"Hey, Shimamura."

I flinched. There was a hardness in Adachi's voice as she called my name.

She slung her bookbag over her shoulder and jerked her chin down the street.

"I gotta go get my bike."

"Huh?" *But you didn't ride your bike today.*

If I'd been thinking clearly, I would've realized that she meant *from the repair shop.*

"See you, uh, tomorrow, I guess." With a wave, she headed off down the street alone.

"Hey!" I called after her.

She glanced back, offered me another wave, and kept going. *Weren't we just talking about going somewhere together? What brought this on?*

"Is she mad or something...?"

Was Adachi throwing a fit because I talked to someone else for five minutes? No, surely that couldn't be it. Maybe she was just too embarrassed to be seen with us and had to leave. *But then again... Well... But what if... Ugh! Forget it! I don't get you, Adachi!*

As I debated whether to go after her, Yashiro turned to me, still smacking her lips. "As payment for the donut, would you like me to explain what just happened?"

"Knock yourself out."

"She's jealous that she didn't get a donut."

"Go home." I flicked my hand at Yashiro in a shooing gesture. *If you were a fish, I'd throw you back.*

Now I had yet another mystery on my plate. Knowing Adachi, she'd probably get over it by tomorrow, but still... I pressed a hand to my forehead and sighed. "Why do interpersonal relationships have to be so complicated? It's just too much work."

"I can relate."

"Somehow I doubt that."

So, yet another weirdo had inflicted themselves upon our town. Would this self-proclaimed time traveler change my life drastically? I had no clue. Life wasn't really something you could change in the first place.

After all, how could any of us alter the future when we didn't even know what it looked like to begin with?

3. Adachi, Questioning

I HAD A DREAM that Shimamura and I kissed.

When I woke up, I was a jumbled mix of emotions. I got so mad at myself that I tousled my hair in frustration. But, eventually, I struck upon something resembling an excuse.

I wasn't gay or whatever. Nor was Shimamura, as far as I knew. I felt guilty for having that kind of dream at all. If she ever found out, she'd probably avoid me—so I needed to keep my mouth shut about it.

When we kissed, it didn't feel like anything, probably because I'd never touched her lips in real life. When our fingers intertwined, though, the dream replicated their softness with perfect accuracy. It was all so real, it felt like someone had dug up my subconscious desires and plastered them on a billboard right in front of my face. I felt sick to my stomach.

We were in Shimamura's room—a place I'd never been in real life, mind you—watching TV. She sat against the wall with her legs spread apart, and I sat between them, leaning back against her. She was smiling at me with this warm, loving expression. Then I turned to her, and our faces were inches apart, and... *AAAAHHH!*

As I reviewed the sequence of events, I screamed internally, and my body broke out in a cold sweat.

The dream was probably just...my brain's way of expressing my desire to be closer friends with Shimamura. I wanted my relationship with her to be "different" compared to her other friends—but just a little. For example, maybe I could call her by her first name while everyone else called her Shimamura. That would be more than enough to make me feel special. But it was a little too late to start calling her something else; it'd just be weird if I tried. And, to be honest, I couldn't remember what her first name even was.

To me, she was just...Shimamura. Something about it felt reassuring, too. Like a big, fluffy security blanket.

So, yeah, I definitely wasn't gay. The kiss didn't even mean anything.

"Nope! Nope, nope, nope...!"

I mean, I wouldn't have said that I'd *never* kiss Shimamura, but I didn't actively *want* to.

Maybe, if she were in a coma, and no one else was around within, say, a three-mile radius, and some all-powerful being told me she wouldn't wake up for a full twenty-four hours...maybe, after hour twenty-three, I'd try it out of sheer boredom. That was the extent of my interest in kissing her, which is to say, basically zero. Zilch.

"Wait... Wouldn't it be less weird if I refused to kiss her under *any* circumstances...?"

But, if the tables were turned, and *she* wanted to kiss *me*, I probably wouldn't refuse. Maybe I'd be scared or confused, but I wouldn't stop her. *Yeah, maybe something's wrong with me.*

I could agonize about the dream all day long, but it wouldn't solve anything. Again, to be clear, I was *not* gay. That said...I could admit to feeling a certain level of possessiveness toward Shimamura.

I just wanted her to prioritize me, that was all.

I wanted to be the first person she thought of when she heard the word "friend."

For a long time, I'd wondered how much Shimamura liked me. Was I on the same level as her other friends, or was I a special case? It was hard to gauge, since she hardly ever talked about other people or even herself. *She thinks she barely knows me? The door swings both ways!*

When it came down to it, all I could really do was ask her. But how could I possibly look her in the eye and say, "Shimamura, how much do you like me?" What if she said "I don't"?

That was the sort of thing my brain occupied itself with as my hand moved automatically to copy down notes in class. I wasn't obsessed with her or anything—I just didn't have much else to worry about.

Third period: math class. There was no point in actually paying attention. I was rusty on the basics, and thus, absolutely none of the class made sense to me. Naturally, this made note-taking even more mind-numbing than usual. Every now and then, I *very briefly* glanced at Shimamura out of the corner of my eye; she was holding a mechanical pencil with a sleepy look on her face.

I didn't realize it until after I started coming back to class, but...there really weren't a lot of opportunities to talk to her while school was in session.

Obviously, we couldn't talk during class, but even during break periods, her desk was too far away for me to walk over without it being awkward. It just felt too... direct. Even when we were both assigned cleanup duty, we always ended up in charge of different areas, so we barely saw each other. That left lunch and after school.

But Shimamura usually spent lunch with Hino and Nagafuji, and being around them always made me pull back. I did want to fit in with them, honestly, but I just couldn't. I wasn't the kind of person who could smile and play nice with everyone; I'd sooner avoid social situations altogether.

Shimamura had figured that out about me, so she never tried to strong-arm me into it. She was perfectly fine doing her own thing without me. But sometimes...at least, in times like these...I wished she would choose me over the others.

So, with lunch out of the question, all that remained was after school. Most of the time, she went straight home as quickly as possible; apparently, she was trying to make up for the classes she missed by studying extra-hard at her house. (In my opinion, she was actually a good kid at heart.) Whenever she went home to study, I did the same.

After that weird dream last night, I found myself too self-conscious to approach her. And Shimamura almost never went out of her way to invite me to anything—that was why I was so startled when she asked me to go to class with her. Thus, most days came and went without a single interaction between us.

We never hung out over the weekends. I only ever saw her on campus, and if we went somewhere else together, it was after school, both of us still in uniform. That was as far as our friendship ever went.

It just felt so...I don't know...*one-sided*.

If you knocked, Shimamura would open the door... but otherwise, she never came out.

Now you may be wondering, what is "Neo-Chinese Cuisine"? Me, I couldn't tell you. If you asked the people who run this place, I bet you they couldn't tell you, either. But that's what they put on the sign out front. An eternal mystery.

For some reason, there were a lot of Taiwanese-owned Chinese restaurants in this town—in this whole region, supposedly—and the one I worked at was no exception. The managers and employees were all Taiwanese; some of them had yet to master the Japanese language. As with any Chinese restaurant, the building exterior made ample use of the color yellow. Plus, the lunch menu was cheap, and the chicken karaage was huge.

This was my part-time workplace. Why did I have a part-time job? Because it seemed like a productive use of my time. Better than sitting around twiddling my thumbs, anyway. Then again, part of me sometimes wondered whether my Sundays and weekday evenings would be better spent on some kind of social life.

Mass-printed menus with photos of some other restaurant's food sat on each table. Day in and day out, customers placed their orders, only to receive end products that looked nothing like the pictures the menu showed. In fact, it was practically a miracle if customers actually got what they asked for.

As with many Chinese restaurants, a bookshelf held manga for customers to read. However, since there was only a smattering of volumes, you couldn't expect to get the whole story. A cheap-looking dragon decoration hung from the ceiling, helping to create a strangely exotic atmosphere.

Granted, working there wouldn't have been so bad if it weren't for the uniform. Why was *I* the only one who had to wear a *cheongsam*? The ankle-length dress was bright blue, with plum-blossom and bamboo-leaf embroidery and a deep slit running up the side, exposing my bare legs. Then again, my school uniform exposed a lot more leg than that... but, for some reason, wearing the *cheongsam* was more embarrassing. Possibly because the fabric was so glossy.

When I asked the boss lady why I was the only female employee expected to wear it, she replied, "Because you're young." Made sense, I guess. I started the job over summer break, so by this point, I was pretty much used to the uniform...but, whenever I thought too hard about it, I kinda wanted to disappear.

A car was already waiting in the parking lot outside, but it was only 4:58, so none of the employees paid the car any mind. These Taiwanese people really seemed to like their strict timeframes. As I gazed out at the pale-white car, I prayed that the restaurant wouldn't get too busy that night.

Two minutes later, at 5:00, my older female coworker (Taiwanese, barely spoke a word of Japanese) walked outside, took down the big "CLOSED" sign, and switched on the neon "OPEN" sign. Only then did the car doors open. It was already getting dark, and naturally this backwater town couldn't afford any highfalutin streetlights, so I couldn't tell how many customers to expect.

My coworker came back inside, followed by a family of four. Before I'd even stopped to look at them, I launched into my usual routine.

"Welcome to—oh."

When I did finally look, however, I stopped dead in my tracks. Standing behind the middle-aged couple...was Shimamura.

She recognized me instantly. "Oh."

I had refused to tell her where I worked, and yet somehow she found me anyway. I knew it was probably just an insane coincidence, but nevertheless, I was stunned.

She gawked at my uniform. "Whoaaa."

I stared at the floor, feeling like a panda on display at the zoo. If anyone else had ogled me like that, I'd have torn them a new one.

Then Shimamura's...mom?...turned to her and asked, "Friend of yours?"

"Yeah, from school," Shimamura replied quickly and curtly, probably because it was her mom asking. For some reason, it delighted me to discover that tiny shift in her attitude.

Evidently, these were Shimamura's parents. Her father was on the chubby side; based on his overall vibe, he seemed like a nice guy. As for her mother, she had slender legs and broad shoulders. *She looks like she works out.*

Lastly, a younger girl—almost certainly the sister she'd mentioned last time we hung out—stood in Shimamura's shadow. Our eyes met. She seemed shyly interested in my *cheongsam*.

"I didn't know you worked here, Adachi. I like your Chinese dress."

"...Table for four, right this way."

I felt my coworkers' eyes on me, so for now, I led the family to a table in the corner. There, Shimamura's parents sat on the left, while Shimamura and her sister sat on the right. Little Shimamura pressed up against her big sister, reaching for the menu. They seemed close.

As I brought out some water and prepared to take their orders, I noticed Shimamura looking at me. "This is why I didn't want you to come," I muttered under my breath. No amount of adjusting would stop the slit from showing off my legs.

"Oh, relax. You're totally rocking the look!" she insisted, grinning in a playful, mischievous sort of way. Though it was rare to see Shimamura smile so unabashedly, that didn't actually feel like a compliment, so much as a fun thing she wanted to say out loud.

"So, you're Adachi-chan, I take it?" Mrs. Shimamura asked. Out of the corner of my eye, I saw Shimamura struggling to keep a straight face.

"Yes, ma'am."

"It's nice to finally meet one of my daughter's friends. Now that she's in high school, she never brings anyone home anymore. Makes me wonder who she's running around with."

"Yeah, ha ha..." I said reluctantly.

"Just ignore her," Shimamura cut in, waving a dismissive hand in her mother's direction.

Relatable.

"So, tell me, are you two in the same class?" Mrs. Shimamura asked.

"Stop it," Shimamura snapped. She thrust her palm forward in a "cease-and-desist" gesture, looking irritated.

"Oh, come on!" Mrs. Shimamura laughed. The way she avoided taking her daughter's complaints seriously kind of reminded me of my own family. Back in junior high, I had been *really* self-conscious. It caused a lot of...problems.

But, the more Shimamura panicked, the easier it became for me to keep my composure.

"So, uh...what's the story with...this...?" I wanted to ask why they were at the restaurant, but couldn't find the words.

Thankfully, Shimamura intuited what I was getting at. "Oh yeah, um, we got some coupons in the mail, so we decided to give the place a try," she explained.

"Oh, gotcha." Silently I cursed the management. Their careless actions had inadvertently led to humiliation for both Shimamura and me.

Today she had tied her hair back in a ponytail, affording her a more "put-together" vibe compared to her usual style. Or did it just seem that way because her younger sibling sat next to her?

Naturally, Little Shimamura hadn't bleached her hair, so it was much darker than her big sister's. That was the color Shimamura's hair would be if she let it grow out... It was a flattering shade, to be sure.

"When you're ready to order, just give me a shout."

I bolted. While talking with Mrs. Shimamura, I'd temporarily forgotten that I was wearing a *cheongsam*, but I couldn't bear to be Shimamura's costumed entertainer any longer. I trusted her not to tell anyone at school, of course. Still, she was the last person I would've wanted to discover me like this.

I walked all the way to the entrance, putting as much distance between myself and Shimamura as physically possible.

"That you friend?" my older coworker asked in her halting Japanese. I nodded slightly. Yes, Shimamura was my friend. That much was undeniable.

Then Little Shimamura peered over at her big sister's menu, pointed, and shouted "Shark fin mushrooms!"

"Don't order that," Mr. Shimamura scolded her.

Personally, I was inclined to agree, since we couldn't actually serve the dish. That was the downside to using a mass-printed menu.

As I watched the Shimamuras interact at the table, I sensed that they were a happy family. I kind of envied that. As for my family, we were pretty...*no frills* with each other. We didn't have much in common; we just lived together because we were blood-related. As you can imagine, my relationship with them was fairly hollow as a result.

All envy aside, however, I did *not* want the Shimamuras to spend all night having a heartwarming family dinner. I wanted them to hurry up and get out of the restaurant. Or I wanted to go home. I tugged on my dress over and over. If only everyone else was wearing the same thing... *Oh god, she just looked at me!* Reflexively, I averted my gaze.

To Shimamura, it probably just seemed as though her friend from class was embarrassed about her outfit. I had more to be embarrassed about than that, though. Every time I looked at her, I remembered the dream I'd had two nights earlier. Once again, I reminded myself that the dream itself was *not* a product of inappropriate feelings. Rather, it was a symptom of the worry spawned from my inability to gauge our friendship's depth—nothing more, nothing less.

But, if someone had asked me to look Shimamura in the eye, I wasn't sure that I could. Maybe under more normal circumstances, when I'd had time to prepare.

Hoping to make the moment more bearable, I attempted to convince myself that this was a little secret the two of us could share...but even that didn't hold water against the indignity of a "Chinese dress." My skin felt like it was on fire.

Mrs. Shimamura beckoned me over. "Adachi-chan!" Evidently, they were ready to order.

"You go now," my coworker told me, clapping me on the shoulder as though it was no big deal.

Closing my eyes, I turned and willed my leaden legs forward. It was time to go make a fool of myself for no reason. Then again, I guess nobody humiliates themselves on purpose.

The next day, I was up in the gym loft. Naturally, I hadn't gone to class; simply put, I was playing hooky. After a week of attending class with Shimamura, I basically felt as though I'd earned a day off. I sat with my back against the wall and zoned out.

When I unfocused my eyes, the world around me seemed to multiply, layering over itself. Some people preferred to keep a clear mind, but me, I enjoyed that fuzzy feeling. I would sit there and go completely zen until I forgot to blink or breathe. It was freeing.

It was still early morning—partway through second period, if I recalled correctly. Below me, I heard the *thud* of a ball bouncing. Rubbing my eyes, I pressed myself against the wall and peered down to the first floor. There, a group of boys were chasing a basketball. Another less-motivated group sat in the corner, talking and laughing. *If I were a guy, I'd probably be down there right now. Same with Shimamura.*

I didn't want to risk making a scene by getting myself caught, so I quickly drew back into safety. Then I put my hand into my bookbag beside me and pulled out my phone. No missed calls, no emails. I tapped around for a while, then put the phone away.

I was no social butterfly, and yet whenever I was bored, I somehow always found myself reaching for my phone. *Guess that's a millennial for you.* I pressed the back of my head against the wall and exhaled quietly.

Nothing bad had happened. I wasn't upset or anything. But after yesterday, I felt lazy, and I knew that even if I went to class, I wouldn't be able to settle down into work mode. Thinking back, that was pretty close to why I'd started skipping school in the first place.

It had been one full week since I last breathed in the stuffy loft air. Taking it into my lungs weighed me down, anchoring me in place; the taste of sheer indolence was strong enough to gag me. *Is this how a nicotine addict feels when they relapse?* I didn't smoke, so I wasn't sure.

Enveloped in the heat and the sounds of sneakers squeaking on the waxy gym floor, my eyelids grew heavy. As a hint of drowsiness washed over my mind, my mouth moved on its own.

"Maybe I'm lying to myself."

I had one other hazy reason to be up here: I hoped Shimamura would notice my absence from the classroom and come looking for me. Admittedly, I felt like a little kid who had run away from home—I wanted someone to care that I was gone. Also, part of me had hoped that she'd be here when I showed up. She wasn't, though.

Was I the only one who cared about what happened yesterday?

I sensed a stark difference in the way she treated me versus how I treated her. No surprise there, of course. The more invested in her I became, the more I worried about my own mental health. Why was I basing every decision I made around Shimamura? Exasperated with myself, I covered my eyes with my hands.

At the rate I was going, it was starting to look as though I had a *crush* on her or something.

A few minutes after the lunch bell rang, I heard someone coming up the stairs, so I exhaled all the laziness from my system and sat up straight. Tempted as I was to look over at the landing, I forced myself to face forward. I could tell from their footsteps that it was a student. Every passing second felt like an eternity.

"Adachi."

I flinched so hard, I felt it in my ears, and timidly turned in the direction of the voice. It was Shimamura, naturally.

"What's up?" I asked, trying to play it cool as I wrestled with mixed feelings of joy and guilt.

"Why don't we eat lunch in the cafeteria for a change?"

She was acting completely normal. Clearly, she wasn't hung up about yesterday. But since she came all the way to the loft to get me, she had to care about me at least a little...or so I chose to tell myself.

"Sure, I don't mind."

I grabbed my bookbag and pushed myself up from the floor. As I dusted my skirt off, I turned in her direction.

This was the Shimamura I was used to—no street clothes, no ponytail. She waited for me to fix my uniform, and then we headed out of the gym together.

As we walked, it occurred to me that we hadn't even said hello to each other. Then again, with us, that was par for the course. Hardly ever said hello, almost never said goodbye.

"Just when I thought she'd cleaned up her act, here we are again!" Shimamura declared out of nowhere in an oddly deep voice, as though she was imitating someone.

"Who's that supposed to be?"

"Our homeroom teacher. He wanted to know why you weren't in class, and I was like, 'How should I know?'" She shrugged her shoulders.

If the teacher had asked her about me, that meant he believed that it was possible she had the answer. And *that* meant he saw the two of us as close friends. *Interesting*.

"You enjoyed that, huh? I didn't think I nailed the impression," Shimamura commented, looking at me with surprise in her eyes.

"Huh…? What are you talking about?" I asked, confused.

"That look on your face," she replied, pointing at my mouth.

I poked my cheeks. Was I really smiling that hard? Yes. Yes, I was. Then I realized what had actually made me smile and low-key wanted to die.

"Aw, c'mon. You don't have to be embarrassed about it."

"Easy for you to say."

Apparently, she thought my shame stemmed from her catching me wearing my emotions on my sleeve. *She has no idea. Thank god.* Massaging my cheeks, I followed behind her as we entered the cafeteria building.

Truth be told, it was my first time setting foot in there. The older students' overwhelming presence made it slightly intimidating for a first-year like me to walk in. Plus, I didn't always feel the need to eat lunch.

As we made our way inside, I hastily scanned the area so I could figure out what I was supposed to do before I made a fool of myself. Evidently the cafeteria used a meal-ticket system; a line of students had formed in front of what appeared to be a ticket machine. We joined that line. On the other side of the blue pillars, a second line led up to the register.

Was this where Shimamura always bought lunch for us? I'd never tagged along with her, so I couldn't be sure, but I saw a vending machine selling mineral water. One soda flavor was sold out; a red light flashed beneath a yellow logo.

We waited in line in complete silence. Personally, I was so overwhelmed by the buzz of the students around us, I could scarcely breathe. I knew that I'd probably feel better if I just thought of something to talk about, but my mind was a blank. For a moment, I stared straight ahead at the back of Shimamura's perfect, slender neck... but then, I got scared, thinking she might turn around and catch me. My only option was to face the other way.

As I waited in line endlessly for my turn, I killed time by taking in the idyllic lunchtime scenery around me. Sunlight glinting sharply off the distant school-building windows. Clouds glowing in the light, with tiny glimpses of blue in the gaps between. The hustle and bustle of the people behind me. The faint smell of food.

Finally, after a long and strenuous test of my endurance, it was our turn at last. Shimamura had gotten her money out well in advance, so she popped it into the machine and promptly ordered the daily special: the Chinese rice bowl. *But you just had Chinese food last night,* I thought. I ordered the same thing.

At the front of the second line, we traded in our meal tickets for the corresponding meals, then paused by the water cooler to grab cups of water. All that remained was to find a place to sit...but the rectangular blue tables were filled with people everywhere we looked. Food and drink in hand, we walked around the entire cafeteria until eventually, mercifully, we spotted an empty table in the corner.

When we sat down, the first thing I did was take a sip of my water. It was room temperature and tasted faintly of metal. Same with the tap water back home. That was why I generally preferred mineral water.

Next, I set my cup down and picked up my chopsticks. Then I felt Shimamura's gaze from across the table, so I looked up, and she giggled.

I froze. "What?"

"Oh, just remembering how cute you looked last night."

Never before had the word "cute" made me blush quite so quickly. I couldn't bear to look Shimamura in the eye. She wore another of those rare, genuine smiles; her teeth showed and everything. I decided my best bet was to try to get back at her.

"You're pretty cute yourself."

"What? Isn't this how I always look?"

My point exactly. But she didn't realize I meant it in the general sense. Instead, she took it as a joke.

For some reason, she seemed to think I was the more attractive one; but, in my opinion, she couldn't have been more wrong. I wanted to tell her that flat-out, but I sensed it would make things weird between us, so I didn't argue the point. Instead, I clicked my chopsticks idly.

"Maybe we should eat there again sometime."

"Stop. Don't you dare." I wasn't messing around, either. If her family started eating at my restaurant all the time, I'd have to find a new job.

"I'm *kidding*. It'd be weird to come see you with my whole family."

"Right? It's kinda embarrassing to have your entire family there."

"Totally."

She paused to say grace, so I followed suit. Truth be told, I generally ate most of my meals alone, so I almost never remembered to do that. Once Shimamura and I started eating, the conversation died. She'd managed to talk and eat at the same time with her family the previous night, but apparently, that wasn't in the cards for us.

I guess it's just different when you're talking to family. I wish I had some kind of special connection with her, too. Like if I was her best friend, or her girlfriend... Okay, maybe not her girlfriend. Probably not. Definitely not.

As I ate, I casually wondered what it would be like to actually date Shimamura. At our age, even if we did find boyfriends, we weren't expected to marry them or start families. In that case, why stick to only dating guys? If we didn't need to get married and have kids, then this seemed like the ideal time to date girls instead. I couldn't see any problems with it.

What am I thinking? Of course there are problems! Just because I was cool with it didn't mean the rest of the world would be, to say nothing of whether *Shimamura* would be. Wait...did that mean the problems with same-sex dating were all external? Was I sincerely fine with it on a personal level? Surely I had some objection. After a moment of contemplation, I thought of one.

If I dated women into adulthood, I would never pass on my genes. My family line would end with me. Sure, one could argue that there were plenty of other people in the world to ensure the human race's overall survival, but what if same-sex dating snowballed into a larger trend? I didn't know what percentage of the population was interested in that, but if the answer was "a lot," the world was in trouble. *That's the danger of being an outlier. It all makes sense now...*

Did I really like Shimamura that much?

I snuck a glance at her over the rim of my bowl. My eyes were drawn to her face, particularly her lips. Her bleached brown hair swayed with her every move, and she wore more layers of makeup than I did, but her eyes looked tired. She ate modestly, with tiny movements.

Before now, I'd never really noticed just how cute she was—but, now that I was conscious of it, suddenly everything about her was *adorable*. For a moment, I found myself entranced. Then I caught myself and hastily shook the thought away.

Good looks aside, what was it about her that made her so special to me?

"Oh, hey! It's Shimamura and Adachi!"

I was so startled, I nearly spilled my food. Setting my bowl back down on the table, I looked up to find two more girls carrying the same lunch we ordered.

"Oh, hey," Shimamura replied.

At that, the girls sat down next to us at the table as if invited. As I recalled, the shorter girl's name was Hino, and the taller one was Nagafuji. Hino happened to have chosen the spot beside me.

"I didn't know you were here," she commented.

"Huh? Oh, uh...yeah." It took me a minute to realize what she meant—I hadn't gone to class, so everyone automatically assumed that I was absent. Right. That still didn't explain why they thought they could barge in on our lunch, though.

"Hey, you," called Nagafuji from across the table.

"Her name's Adachi. Don't be rude," Hino shot back, pointing her chopsticks at Nagafuji.

Nagafuji laughed. "Oh, who cares! Anyway, Adachi-san, I wanted to tell you..."

"Yes?"

She smiled softly. "Good morning!"

Uh...little late for that, don't you think?

Then again, it was technically proper etiquette. Communication 101: start with a greeting, and go from there. Still, Nagafuji seemed a bit out of sync with the rest of us.

"Um...good morning."

Oddly enough, I picked up distinctly ditzy vibes from her, though she seemed intelligent and mature at first glance. Then she noticed that I had my bookbag. "Did you just get here?"

"Nah, I was playing hooky," I answered honestly.

"Whoaaaa," she and Hino murmured in unison. *Not sure what's so "whoa" about it, but okay.*

"So, what are you guys doing in here?" Shimamura asked them. "Normally, you both bring your own lunch, don't you?"

"Mama overslept," Hino answered, wiggling her chopsticks. She had a habit of gesturing with her hands when she talked; was she fidgety, or just overly energetic?

Then it was Nagafuji's turn. "There wasn't a whole lot in the fridge."

At first, this seemed like a weird answer...until I realized that she probably made her own lunches.

Hino turned to me. "Her family runs a butcher shop," she explained, pointing her chopsticks in Nagafuji's direction.

"Oh," I replied curtly, since I didn't really see what that had to do with anything.

"The other day, I stopped by and asked her to sell me some titty meat. And you know what she did? She punched me! Terrible service, that butcher shop!"

"Papa told me I'm allowed to punch people as long as they aren't customers."

And they think I'm *the delinquent? At least* I've *never gone around punching anyone!*

"Say, Shima*moo*ra-san, wanna have a bite of my food?" Hino asked, holding a carrot slice in her chopsticks. *Why would she want your food when she ordered the exact same thing as you? You're not going to make her eat off your utensils, are you?*

"We both got the same thing, Hino."

"So what? Who cares?! C'mon!" She set her carrot on top of Shimamura's bowl.

"You just want me to eat your carrots, don't you? Hey! Not you too, Nagafuji!"

Meanwhile, Nagafuji had silently transferred all her carrots to Shimamura's bowl. For a second, I contemplated joining in myself. Then Shimamura shot me an exasperated grin, a look I returned in kind for some reason.

I didn't mind the lighthearted atmosphere Hino and Nagafuji brought whenever they showed up. In fact, it was actually kind of fun in a way that made me nostalgic for elementary school... However, part of me was decidedly not happy about them sitting down with us.

Shimamura and I hadn't hung out by ourselves in a long time, and right when we finally had the chance, these two showed up to crash the party. Truth be told, their presence felt...*wrong* somehow. That was probably why I grinned back at Shimamura—to hide my discomfort.

"Nice to see you actually smile for a change," Shimamura teased me.

"Wow, rude." *I'm a human being, not a statue. And didn't you just catch me smiling earlier? I'm a sunny little sunflower over here. Okay, not really.*

If anything, it felt like *she* was the one who hardly ever smiled. *And I'm not thinking about that fake smile you wear in social settings.*

So, what was it that Shimamura actually enjoyed doing? I'd tried asking her flat-out a couple times in the past, but all I got was "Not much" or "Good question" as she tilted her head in contemplation.

Our happy little lunchtime came to an end. Across the cafeteria, students jumped to their feet to put away their trays, and we followed suit.

"What's your plan for this afternoon?" Shimamura asked me as we stacked our dirty bowls on top of each other. I was in no mood to walk back to the gym by myself. Plus, I *did* have my bookbag.

"I'm going to class."

"Gotcha." Her voice sounded a little giddy...or was I reading too much into it? Either way, it made my heart flutter.

Side by side, she and I walked a short distance behind Hino and Nagafuji. Feeling ever-so-slightly rebellious, I lowered my voice so the other two wouldn't hear me. "Hey, Shimamura?"

"Hmm?"

"Can I come over to your house today?" I asked, mildly nervous.

She cocked her head. "What for?"

"I dunno...because I'm bored?"

From the look on her face, I could tell she wondered why I chose her house, of all places, to entertain myself when there was a whole town to explore. That dubious expression always made me a little uncomfortable—it felt as though she was judging me for being weird. *Nah, I'm probably just overthinking it.*

"I don't mind, but my house isn't exactly fun or anything. Plus, my sister... Eh, I guess it's fine." Evidently she didn't feel like getting into it, but I sensed that she was worried that her sister would be annoying or something. "Seriously, my house is nothing to write home about."

"That's okay." I nodded without looking at her. I wasn't expecting anything super special; I just wanted to be able to say that I'd been there. I wanted to be one step ahead of her other friends. By no means was I just trying to get some time alone with her.

Shimamura's house. Shimamura's room.

The memory of the dream threatened to rear its ugly head. Desperately I shook it from my mind.

After school, Shimamura followed me out to the bike parking area.

"Oh, your bike's fixed?"

"Yeah."

I recalled last week's events. Thinking of them always

managed to piss me off, so I'd tried my best to suppress the memories.

Somehow that astronaut girl was still a total mystery, even after I met her in person. Who *was* she? If it were me, I would have ignored her and kept walking. But Shimamura could talk to anyone as though they were normal. In that respect, she was very...neutral. The thought that I was on level footing with that freaky astronaut girl had set me off.

Fortunately, Shimamura didn't seem upset about it.

"Want a ride?" I kicked my back wheel.

"Heck yeah. Let me put this here." She set her bookbag in my basket, put a hand on my shoulder, and hopped on.

Personally, I would rather have waited until we were past the school gates, but I wasn't about to stop her, so instead I started pedaling. With the total weight now doubled, the first few seconds were pretty rough, but it got easier and easier as we picked up momentum.

"You don't have work today?"

"Nope. Not till tomorrow."

I didn't want to risk a teacher flagging us down to yell at us for "reckless behavior" or whatever, so I pedaled as fast as I could to get us off campus ASAP. Together, Shimamura and I sailed through the gates and down the street.

"My house is the other way."

"Crap, that's right." Without thinking, I'd automatically steered in the direction of my own house. I pulled a hard U-turn and headed back in the opposite direction, briefly passing the school gates once again.

"So, you're really coming over to my house?"

"Yeah...? Is that bad?"

If she didn't want me to, then I wouldn't. But Shimamura didn't answer the question. Instead, she asked me, "That Chinese dress you were wearing... Did you bring it from home?"

Where did that come from? And what kind of question is it?

"Uh, no? Obviously?"

"Then how come no one else was wearing one?"

"Because... You know."

"No, I don't know. Why?"

"Because I'm the youngest or whatever."

"That, and you look so good in it."

"I wouldn't say that." *I guess she likes my uniform... Then again, does Shimamura ever really like ANYTHING?*

As I pedaled down the road, I looked up at her, and our eyes met.

"Stop that! You have to watch where you're going!" Shimamura insisted, pointing ahead of us. But I kept looking, reminded of the other time we'd done this a while back. Her expression stiffened in a way I'd never seen before. "Seriously, come on!"

These days she fills my every waking moment, and I don't know why.

"Here we are, milady. Welcome to the House of Shimamura," I announced as we pulled up out front.

"Sounds like something Hino would say," Shimamura replied. Thinking back to the conversation we had over lunch, I was inclined to agree.

I locked up my bike, then turned to the house. It had a blue-tiled roof and a hardwood deck leading into the yard, though the wood had rotted in places in its old age. Clean laundry fluttered idly on the drying rack.

This was my first time going over to a friend's house as a high school student, and for all I knew, it was possibly the last.

Shimamura unlocked the front door, opened it, and looked down at the little shoes lined up against the inner wall. "Yep, she's here," she murmured, removing her shoes and setting them next to what I suspected were her sister's. I followed suit and added mine to the procession. Then we set off down the hallway, past the stairs.

"Your room's on the first floor?"

"Is that weird? I guess most people have an upstairs bedroom."

I couldn't say for sure, but *I* certainly had an upstairs bedroom, as did most of the kids whose houses I visited in elementary school. Maybe that was the trend back when our houses were built.

At the end of the hall, Shimamura pointed to a door. "This is my room."

She twisted the knob, and the very next instant, a little voice shouted.

"Oneechan! Welcome...home...?"

It was Little Shimamura. Her enthusiasm at seeing her sister quickly petered out when she realized I was with her.

She sat on the floor playing a video game, her *randoseru* backpack lying forgotten in one corner. Specifically, she was playing one of those motion-control games where you swing the controller around. Ping-pong, by the looks of it. Onscreen, a little cartoon character jumped for joy; her "opponent" had scored a point against her while she was distracted.

"Thanks," Shimamura replied curtly, then gestured to me. "This is my friend. You remember that we saw her yesterday?"

"Uh-huh."

Little Shimamura turned off the game console and started to tidy up. Once she was done, she headed out of the room. It seemed an awful lot like she'd been waiting for her big sister to get home so they could play together... My chest ached. She reminded me of a smaller version of myself, right down to the way she bolted at the first sign of conflict.

"I feel bad for intruding."

"Nah, it's fine. She's just shy, that's all."

Evidently, her oneechan was clueless. *If I see her again before I leave, I should apologize,* I thought. Then I realized I was still standing awkwardly in the doorway.

This was Shimamura's room.

It was nothing like the room I'd dreamed about... Not that I expected otherwise, obviously, because that would be stupid. The shape and size, the wall color, the view from the window—all completely different.

It occurred to me that my dream had been really detailed. *Abnormally* detailed. Normally there'd be fuzzy parts, but this one hadn't had any.

In my fantasy—I mean, my dream—Shimamura's room had pale-blue wallpaper and pastel curtains. Her bed was against the wall, next to a desk. Across from the bed was a TV, and the sunset tinted the view through the second-story window scarlet. The two of us were sitting on the bed, Shimamura with her back against the wall, me leaning up against her.

In reality, her room had white walls, and instead of a bed, there were two futons on the floor. That surprised me more than anything else. The TV was next to the window, and on the TV stand beneath it was a stack of Blu-rays, as well as the game console from earlier. The bookshelf was filled with what I assumed was Little Shimamura's manga collection, but I saw a ping-pong tactics guide tucked away in the back. That put a smile on my face.

Lastly, two ancient study desks sat side by side. They encapsulated what my dream had gotten wrong—I never once imagined that Shimamura shared a room with her kid sister. At least, I don't think I did. But it was just a dream, so it didn't matter. It wasn't my fault.

My dream also failed to anticipate the fish tank by the door, its residents swimming around lazily.

"You like fish?" I asked.

"Hino caught them and gave them to me, but my sister likes to feed them, so they're basically hers now. She's the pet caretaker at school, too," Shimamura explained, grinning.

"*Pet caretaker*! That takes me back," I laughed. "I didn't know they still did that."

"Apparently so, yeah. Anyway..." She set her bookbag on her desk and plopped down on top of her futon. Then she grabbed the yellow cushion Little Shimamura had just been sitting on and tossed it at me. "Here."

I caught it and looked down at it. The cushion cover featured a black cat and a white cat, mascots for a delivery company, holding hands. I dropped the cushion to the floor and settled down onto it.

"So, what now?" Shimamura asked, sitting with her legs outstretched. Apparently, she wanted me to decide how we were going to kill time.

Bored, she picked up the remote and turned the TV on, then navigated from the AV channel to a regular channel. A show came onscreen—a fairly old one, judging from the picture quality—and I realized that I recognized it. It was a re-run of a show I had watched maybe once a year or so back when I was little. *They still air this?* I laughed to myself as I watched the tanned male lead perform. The show always used to air right after my favorite anime, and I watched it just because I was bored and it was on. I still remembered all the plot beats.

"I can't believe they still air this," Shimamura sighed. Apparently we were of the same mind, and it comforted me to discover another thing we had in common, no matter how small.

However, I felt my eyes wander restlessly. I lightly smacked my temple, trying to knock some sense back into myself. I knew it was stupid to conflate dreams with reality, but...we were sitting too far apart. It just didn't feel right.

"Hey, uh, Shimamura?"

"Hmm?" Her eyes were on the TV screen. She pulled her socks off and tossed them away from the futon onto the floor.

My stomach clenched as my brain screamed at me not to say it. But then I said it.

"I was wondering, um, if I could sit with you, like, between your legs or something."

God, listen to me. I sound like a total weirdo.

"Huh? Sure, I don't mind."

You don't mind? Yeah, right—wait, what? What? Am I dreaming again? She agreed so readily, it threw me for a loop.

As she spread her legs, her expression didn't shift in the slightest. Hesitantly, timidly, I crawled over and settled between them.

I looked down and saw her legs right there. Suddenly I was lightheaded and dizzy. But I knew I couldn't just throw myself against her, so instead I stayed perfectly upright, sitting with my legs crossed, keeping a bit of distance between us. However, resting my full weight on my hips made my tailbone hurt...and then my whole body started to shake.

"What are you doing?"

"Well..."

As I struggled to voice my discomfort, she fixed me with a suspicious look. "My sister does this all the time. It's not weird, right?"

Apparently, she had no qualms treating me the exact same way as her little sister. I wasn't sure whether that was a good thing or a bad thing, but I felt something hot welling in my chest.

"No, of course not..." I lied, afraid that she would kick me away if I said otherwise. Was I taking advantage of her? Or was it actually not that weird? I had no idea.

If I turned my head even slightly, Shimamura's face would come into view. Merely imagining it was enough to make my ears burn red. *What is* wrong *with me? Why am I so self-conscious?* I scarcely heard the TV over my own internal screaming. My ears felt as though they were literally *on fire*—and I was terrified that Shimamura would notice.

"Gotcha!"

"Whoa!"

She must have sensed how uncomfortable I was, because she grabbed my shoulders and pulled me backward.

That caught me completely off-guard, and I slumped against her with my entire weight, swinging my arms as I fell. She was shorter than me, and yet somehow, we fit perfectly together—almost like I'd actually become her little sister. Now her face was directly above mine; she looked down at me with a blank expression, as though it was totally fine.

I straightened up slightly, and she disappeared behind me. "Rrgh," she growled, seemingly annoyed at my superior height.

Frankly, it was a huge relief to have something to lean against. I relaxed, splaying my legs out atop the blanket, and exhaled. The more closely my reality approached my dream, the more vertigo I felt. Drawing my knees to my chest, I felt Shimamura's presence behind me, separated by the insurmountable wall known as my back.

"Do you have a...boyfriend or whatever?"

My lips puckered slightly. For some reason I felt *compelled* to ask her. Looking back, I think this was when I started acting on autopilot.

"What do you think?" she retorted cynically. I knew she didn't mean anything by it, but it still irked me.

"No...?"

"Bingo. Didn't we just have this conversation the other day?"

"Did we...?" My brain wasn't functioning properly, so I couldn't remember.

"What about you? No boyfriend?"

"Nope. Same as you."

"Gotcha," she replied offhandedly.

She probably just asked because it was the polite thing to do. *Yeah, that's gotta be it. That's just how she is.* No matter how random the question, she would give me her answer, and then the conversation would end. She never felt the need to talk about anything more than strictly necessary. At least, not with me.

If the average friendship was a staircase, then ours was an M.C. Escher painting. I couldn't help but wonder if I'd be climbing those stairs forever.

At that thought, I turned slightly, and Shimamura entered my field of vision, her face mere inches from mine. Just like in the dream. Then our eyes met.

"What?" she asked. By this point, even she was starting to think I was acting strange. She was right, of course. I was being an extreme weirdo about the whole thing.

My collarbone ached. Normally people would say their chest or something ached, but for me, it was the bone itself. I could feel it creaking as though it wanted to pop right out of my body. Why? Probably because I was holding my neck at a weird angle. It hurt so bad, it felt like my whole head might fall off.

What can I do to remedy this situation? I asked myself. Then an idea came to me.

"I really like you, you know?"

Wait, what? Hold the phone—what? What did I almost say just now? Wait—did I say it for real? I didn't, did I? But what would she do if I did? What would happen?

"Hmm?" Shimamura cocked her head at me. Apparently, she hadn't heard anything. My throat felt like it was closing up. The corners of my eyes burned.

"I...I think I like you."

But the only sound I produced was a rasping breath, like a chill wind passing through a dark and dreary tunnel. I couldn't speak. My whole ribcage throbbed painfully in time with my heart, almost as though my entire body was *begging* me not to say it. Unable to blink, my eyes started to ache in my skull as they stared back at Shimamura, who looked at me dubiously. Every movement made me flinch.

"I...I think maybe I have feelings for you. But it's just a maybe. It feels like...like I love you."

Why do I keep trying to say it?! I felt my whole jaw quiver as self-loathing washed over me. *This is so stupid. I can't do this. I'm an idiot.*

My memories and my consciousness wriggled like two separate worms until finally, after an eternity, their paths crossed at last.

This is...this is the dumbest thing I've ever done in my life.

Dumbfounded, Shimamura stared at me for a moment. Then her mouth began to move—slowly, hesitantly, as though it were her first time using it.

"Uhhh...you okay...? Are you still breathing? Your face is, like, *really* red."

Then she reached for my lips...and that was the final straw that set me off. A flood of bright-white light blurred my vision—and the next thing I knew, I was on my feet and bolting for the door. Meanwhile, for some reason, I calmly noted my creaking arms and aching head with the clinical interest of an outside observer.

"Wait, don't go...!" Shimamura called. But she showed no sign of actually coming after me, so I left her behind, stumbling on legs so numb that I wasn't confident I'd even be able to ride my bike.

At home, I slammed my face into my pillow and writhed, clutching my head. My memory of the ride home was so vague, it felt as though I'd simply teleported here...but from the intense pain in my legs, I knew I must've pedaled like mad the entire time.

I'd accidentally left my bookbag back in Shimamura's room, but I was in no mood to retrieve it.

"Hnnnnn...!"

Facedown in the pillow, I let out a long groan. Every bead of sweat that trickled down my face seemed to ask, "What's gotten into you?" Whimpering like a baby, I paused to pull off my uniform jacket. Then it was right back to whimpering.

"Whaddafa...*whaddafaaa*...!"

I was so distressed, I was inventing new words. Every time I tried to remember what I'd said, I started shrieking. My head felt like it was splitting apart at the scalp. My breath hitched as tears pricked at the corners of my eyes.

When I finally lifted my head again, there was still plenty of daylight left. As despair dug into my eye sockets, I cursed the sun for being so slow.

"Hnnnnn...my neck hurts... Owww...!"

Something fluttered around in my chest, shadowy and scorching hot. Something I couldn't force back down. I was awash in a waterfall of emotional torment—I wanted it to end, and yet at the same time, I desperately *didn't*.

I could only pray that the world wouldn't come to an end when the sun rose tomorrow.

4. The Isosceles Triangle

IT WAS THE FIRST TIME I'd ever made someone run away at full speed.

After Adachi was gone, I turned back to the TV. There was a small indentation in the blanket between my legs where she'd been sitting. Puzzled, I thought back over the events leading up to her departure—the way her face grew more and more flushed until she was redder than a tomato, followed by the moment right at the end when the color gradually drained again. What *was* that? It seemed as though she was struggling to say something... but what?

"What if..."

No, that can't be it...can it?

Then my eight-year-old sister entered the room.

"Shabadaba!"

If I had been born male, my parents would have given me my own room by now, but because my sister and I were both girls, they shrugged their shoulders and left us as-is. Granted, they put a heater and a fan in the storage room next door in case I ever needed to stay up late to study, but those didn't exactly make the storage room any less dusty.

"She's gone, huh?" my sister asked, glancing around the room. Once she confirmed that Adachi was nowhere to be seen, she plopped down in front of the TV in the corner and grabbed a Wii controller.

Video games AGAIN? I thought as I watched her. But then she turned to me.

"Play with me, *Neechan*!"

"Ugh..."

She loved to play those games, even though she totally sucked at them. But I knew she'd get pissy with me if she lost, so whenever I played against her, I always had to make sure I didn't really try. Hence, I was never particularly enthusiastic about playing...but I was especially unenthusiastic after what just happened.

"Let's do it!"

Without even waiting for a response, she switched on the TV, navigated to the AV channel, and powered on the console. Evidently, she was raring to go. I grabbed the second controller reluctantly.

At that, my sister moved to sit right between my legs, resting her back against me. Before today, I wouldn't have thought anything of it, but now it reminded me of Adachi. My heart ached.

Was it weird to sit like this? Why else would Adachi act the way she did?

"Your friend sure went home quick," my sister commented.

"Yep," I replied offhandedly, resting my chin on top of her head. Adachi's visit was so brief, it was like, *why even bother?*

"Did you guys have a fight?"

"Umm...actually, I'm not sure."

Today my sister chose a competitive puzzle game—one where brightly colored bead-looking things descended from the top of the screen, and you had to group them by color to make them disappear. The ideal strategy was to trigger a big chain reaction, but usually we could get a chain of two or three without much forethought.

Belatedly, I realized I should have suggested that Adachi play something like this with me instead. Story of my life—hindsight always loved to kick me when I was down. My problem was, I never bothered to put those late realizations to good use. Even if the exact same scenario happened a second time, I'd probably do the same things all over again. I just didn't care enough to try to learn from my mistakes.

When Adachi asked how I spent my weekends, I'd struggled to give her an answer. I didn't really have many responses available to me—I never played video games by myself, nor did I read many books, nor did I go see movies. Whenever I went shopping, it was only to buy seasonal clothes. Most of the time, I just sat around and spaced out. That was it.

Every now and then, I'd look down at my hands and realize, *My fingers are so thin and flimsy.* It always made me feel sick to my stomach. What about now, though? Had they tapered off and atrophied?

Adachi was so freaking *opaque.* I couldn't work up the willpower to figure her out.

By the time I realized I was supposed to be *using* my fingers, not staring at them, my sister had already beaten me. I felt her jubilation under my chin. *Now's the time.*

I pulled away for a moment and readied my index finger. "Hey," I said.

She turned to look—and bumped straight into my finger. I'd meant to do this to Adachi, but she never got distracted enough for me to try. Nevertheless, I needed to do it to *somebody*...and my kid sister was the perfect schmuck. *Way to go, dummy.*

"Headbutt attack!" she roared, slamming her skull into my chin.

"Gah!" Pain shot up to my temples as my whole jaw went numb.

Naturally, that transgression did *not* go unpunished.

After what had happened the previous day, I had a feeling Adachi would come to the gym loft...so that's where I went, hoping to beat her to the punch. I waited and waited, and then the bell for first period rang.

"Wait, what?"

No sign of her.

I gazed at the clock for a while, its hour and minute hands pointing right at 9:00 while the second hand carried on. Eventually, I came to the conclusion that Adachi had chosen to sleep in.

We hadn't explicitly agreed to meet up here today, so why was I so shocked by her absence? I pondered this question as I curled into a ball and rolled around the floor. It was starting to feel like she really wasn't going to show. *What did I ever do to piss you off? God, you're so dramatic.*

I sat up, grabbed my bookbag, and pulled out my phone. I was going to email her about it.

We'd exchanged contact info way back when we first met, but we hardly ever went out of our way to get in touch. After all, our conversations never lasted very long in person, so how could we possibly have anything to call or message each other about? Well, now I *did* have something to say. But how to phrase it? My fingers fell still as I brainstormed.

"Why did you leave yesterday?"

Too direct. Over text, it would read like I was angry with her. I needed something softer—something she'd be more inclined to actually respond to.

"Hmm..."

Something told me that all I really needed to do was get a conversation going, and the whole issue would clear itself up. Anything would work. In the end, I went with *"How's it going, friendo?"*

At least I sounded happy. *Aaaand sent! Now we wait.*

I placed my phone on top of my bag—then remembered that I hadn't set it on vibrate, so I fixed that. Somehow, I'd completely forgotten that I was supposed to be skipping class. *Gotta stay quiet.*

As I ran my fingers through my hair, I pursed my lips. *What if Adachi stops coming to school? Would that be my fault? What did I even do to set her off in the first place?*

It felt as though my pet cat had gotten herself stuck in a tree. I never prompted her to do it, and it was entirely her responsibility, but that didn't change the fact that she was trapped. If I cared about helping her, then I needed to forego the blame game and get up there.

If I could've gotten one message to Adachi, it would've been, "Don't give up on your whole life over this one tiny conflict." But I could almost hear her asking, "Well then, what *am* I allowed to give up over?"

Beats me.

"Don't be a coward, Adachi," I whispered.

But, in the end, that coward didn't reply to me all morning...and then lunch rolled around.

Partway through lunch break, I wandered into the classroom. I wasn't strutting or anything, just walking normally, but nevertheless I somehow attracted a bit of attention from my classmates. Anyone I made eye contact with quickly averted their gaze. *Really? You're scared of me? Pathetic.*

Of course, you might wonder if this meant my sister was right to try to walk all over me, but that's a question for another time.

Spotting the only two people who reliably weren't afraid of me, I made a beeline for them.

"Oh ho ho," Hino smirked. "I didn't know you were here! Wait... Isn't that the exact same thing I said yesterday?" Pinching a piece of onion between her chopsticks, she tilted her head pensively.

"It sure is," I replied, availing myself of the closest empty chair and taking a seat. Today, Hino and Nagafuji had once again brought lunches from home; their bento boxes were open on the desk in front of them. Hino's lunch consisted mostly of stewed meat and potatoes with rice—probably just leftovers from dinner the previous night. As for Nagafuji, her lunchbox was packed full of rolled omelet. It looked delicious.

"Gimme some," I begged.

"I'm ignoring you," she replied with a straight face.

Wow, rude! You gave me your carrots yesterday! Then again, knowing her, she'd probably already forgotten about that by now. *Maybe she washes her hair so hard, she gives herself short-term memory loss. Whatever.*

I glanced over at the door, where Adachi's empty seat stood out like a sore thumb.

"Adachi's not here, huh?"

"Nope. She's absent today," Hino answered.

"She is?" Nagafuji cocked her head in confusion—no surprise there. But, as it turned out, there was more to the story.

"Apparently, she's got a bad cold."

"Aha! So, she's having a fake sick day!"

What a relief. I'd been a tiny bit worried that Adachi might have gotten into a terrible accident on her way home from my house or something. Evidently not.

"I saw you both absent and figured you two were up in the gym loft again," Hino commented.

"Nope, just one of us," I replied, holding up my index finger. "We're not attached at the hip, you know."

"You're not? Because you sure seem like you're all over each other constantly," Nagafuji remarked, her phrasing extremely questionable.

"No, we aren't," I insisted. Meanwhile, the idea that these outside observers saw Adachi and me that way had me panicking internally. To be fair, we'd had our share of physical interactions. Holding hands, sitting together... Maybe we weren't "all over each other," but we were certainly intimate. *I'm only doing it because Adachi wants to,* I thought, before catching myself. *If I'm letting her do it, then clearly I don't have a problem with it.*

"Have you eaten, Shimaa-chan?"

"I'm not your 'Shimaa-chan.' Anyway...come to think of it, no, I haven't."

My mother didn't make lunch for me. She knew I always skipped class, so if I'd asked her, she'd probably have laughed in my face. But it was entirely my fault for slacking off, so I couldn't exactly complain. As for Adachi, she'd never brought lunch to school, either. She'd mentioned previously that she didn't really get along with her parents, so maybe that made sense.

Back when we first met, I thought she was a lot more aloof and serious. I soon learned that wasn't the case. Still, every now and then, I caught glimpses of her pessimistic side—her "dark side," perhaps I should say.

"Gotcha," Hino replied. "Well, I bet you're hungry... Here, say ahh."

Once again, as with yesterday, it was carrots. *Maybe you should just tell your parents you don't like carrots... On second thought, you've probably already tried that.*

Meanwhile, Nagafuji stared down at her bento box, biting her lip, her chopsticks hovering timidly over each dish in turn. "I can't do it... There's nothing I hate in here!"

"What am I, your human garbage disposal?"

"Noooo, we love you! Here, have an omelet."

"Yay!"

I decided that this made up for everything else they put me through on a regular basis.

Cleanup time rolled around. I stood in the hallway, broom in hand, just staring into space. Every now and then, when nobody was looking, I checked my phone notifications. No email from Adachi. But I was getting bored of waiting, so I decided to send her another one.

"I wanna come over to your house after school today. Is that cool?"

No reply...but I trusted that Adachi would be nice enough to let me in once I got there. Probably.

After lunch, I sat in class, wondering why Adachi hadn't replied.

Possibility #1: she was straight-up ignoring me.

Possibility #2: she was really struggling to decide what to say in her reply.

Lastly, possibility #3: she hadn't checked her inbox yet. This possibility seemed the most likely of the three.

I generally didn't care about most things, but even I would've been a little offended by #1. Then after a few days, I'd get over myself, and it'd be back to business as usual. I knew it'd repulse people to know that about me, though, so I didn't intend on ever telling anyone.

I still had the little map Adachi had drawn for me last time; it was folded up and tucked away in my bookbag. I reached in and found it almost immediately. It would be a long walk, but if she wasn't going to answer my emails, then she hadn't really left me any other option. I was sure we could work it all out once we started talking.

Something told me that it was stupid to put in so much effort for something that was supposed to come naturally. This felt like too much work. But after the final bell rang, and I passed through the school gates, I found myself walking in the opposite direction from my house. Knowing me, I'd probably stop caring after a few minutes. It wasn't like I had anything better to do with my time.

At some point during this objective self-analysis, I looked up at the blanket of clouds above me. Not a single patch of blue sky was to be seen. It was colder today, too. Maybe now, at the end of October, the weather was finally synchronizing with the season.

The summer heat had *really* worn out its welcome this year. Every day we spent in the gym loft was sweaty and miserable. But as the temperature steadily sank, I had to wonder—would we ever go back? Or was it time for us to leave the nest?

As I walked through a residential neighborhood, I passed a group of grade school kids, their shrill little voices screaming and laughing without a care in the world. At least one of them was blowing into a recorder—maybe a music test was coming up. *Must be nice,* I thought as I watched them, though I wasn't actually all that jealous. You know me—I was too much of a good kid for that.

"Greetings."

"Huh? Wha—?" I turned in the direction of the sudden voice—and jumped backward, my eyes nearly bulging out of my skull.

Standing beside me was a small girl. A weird one. How could I tell, you ask? Her hair. Her hair was *sky blue*. It startled me so badly, I froze like a statue.

Blue hair. No, I wasn't hallucinating, and no, it wasn't a trick of the light. It was her natural hair color. Its strands were floating of their own accord, and radiating little blue...*particles*. And, for some reason, their owner had chosen to interact with *me*.

WHY?

"Uh...have we met?" I asked.

"What's this? You don't recognize me?"

She tilted her head back and forth. Then, after a moment, she took off running down the street. She disappeared around the corner of a distant house...and, a few minutes later, she reappeared. This time she wore a helmet, its visor reflecting daylight directly into my eyes. Now I understood. It was Yashiro. She just wasn't wearing her space suit.

"This is what you look like?"

"Krrrssshhh…krrsshh…krrrssshhh…"

Apparently, all that running had left her out of breath. Unable to stand the helmet for a moment longer, she pulled it off again, and the crazy blue hair made its return.

Once again, her hair threw me for a loop. It was so conspicuous, it seemed to have its own distinct outline, like it existed on another plane of reality. Upon further inspection, Yashiro had a very pretty face, too. Her eyes and eyelashes were the same brilliant blue shade, almost as though the "particles" in her hair circulated through her entire body, painting it all with the same brush. The particles seemed fragile, yet magical—strong and weak at the same time.

"I would've liked it if you'd recognized me from my voice. That way I wouldn't have needed this thing." She gave the helmet a pat as she cradled it under one arm. Frankly, her voice sounded a lot different now that it wasn't so muffled.

In place of her space suit, she wore a sleeveless dress that accentuated her pale, petite body, and sneakers with a logo I couldn't identify. No socks. Oh, and she stood with her hand on her hip.

At her age, she would've looked right at home with a *randoseru* backpack slung over her shoulders, but she wasn't carrying one.

"Now that my face is ready, I wanted to show you. Thoughts?"

"Don't ask me," I replied evasively.

Upon even further scrutiny, I realized that her lips sparkled ever-so-faintly blue—the kind of color that couldn't possibly be lipstick. I pressed a finger to them experimentally.

"Mm?"

I pulled back and looked down at my finger. Nothing. All that remained were little floating sparkles...but they quickly faded away. I stared in disbelief, my eyes as wide as saucers. Now I was really, *really* tempted to grab her by the hair and demand some answers.

"I designed it to resemble an Earthling's."

"Should I be offended? Also, uh...what happened to your space suit?" *And where did you go get your helmet from?*

"Hmmm..." She pressed a finger to her forehead. "I'm afraid so. I had imagined everyone on Earth would wear a space suit, but thus far, I haven't seen any."

"Yeah, you're not going to see one anytime soon." *Except maybe on TV.*

"So, that's why—uh oh!"

She clapped a hand to her mouth and jumped up and down on the spot. Then she reached out her free hand and patted me on the cheek.

"What are you doing?"

"We can't let anyone overhear us, so I need you to lend me your ear."

"Ooookay..."

Apparently, she was reaching for my *ear*, not my cheek. *What was she going to do, grab it and pull? What a goblin.*

I squatted down to Yashiro's eye level. As she leaned in, her particles enveloped my nose, carrying her scent toward me almost visibly. Up close, her face dazzled me, as though every inch glowed somehow. The longer I looked at it, the more drawn in I felt...and the more fearful I became that it would consume me entirely.

She drew her lips to my ear. "I'm going to whisper now."

I didn't need the warning, but okay.

"The truth is, I'm an alien from the future."

"Yeah, I know. You told me your little 'story' last time."

That at least explained why she didn't want anyone to overhear—they'd probably think she was a few corn dogs shy of a picnic. But, considering her ethereal appearance, I was starting to believe her.

"If the Earthlings find out I'm an alien, they will surely dissect me."

"That's a little presumptuous, don't you think?"

Back when I was really little, my mom and I watched this TV show where NASA or whoever revealed some alien dissection footage. My mom was laughing hard the whole time. Now I understand why, of course, but at the time I was convinced that she had to be psychotic.

"Thus, I decided my mission required different clothes in order for me to avoid attracting attention."

Having explained fully, Yashiro stepped backward, out of my bubble. *Yeah, yeah, cool story. Now wipe that smug smirk off your face.*

"I hate to break it to you, but you still attract *plenty* of attention."

Unsurprisingly, almost every grade schooler in our vicinity stared at her as they walked past. She stuck out so badly, she looked as though she'd been Photoshopped into reality.

Then I noticed her unusual hairstyle—a bow tied without the help of any hair accessories. It was gorgeous, reminiscent of running water shaped perfectly into a ribbon, or perhaps a butterfly from a magical kingdom. *Hold on a minute. Is it SUPPOSED to be that tight?*

"Doesn't that hurt your scalp?"

"I inadvertently tied it so tightly that I'm unable to loosen it."

I attempted to pick at the knot. She yelped in pain.

Yashiro might have looked like an otherworldly entity on the outside, but on the inside, she wasn't much different from my little sister. They were the same height, too, come to think of it. *Maybe they'd be good friends... On second thought, maybe not. My sister would probably take one look at Yashiro's hair and run for the hills.*

She grabbed me by the sleeve and lifted my hand to her nose. "You must be on your way home from school. You don't smell quite so wonderful today."

By "wonderful," I assumed she referred to the donut smell from last time. She was pulling my cuff so hard, my blazer threatened to slip down my shoulder. "Unhand me, wench!" I demanded in a theatrical voice as I extricated myself from her grip.

"Noooo!" she wailed feebly, spinning like a top as she whirled away.

What a good sport. You know, I'm starting to think she's not actually an alien.

When she returned, she began to scrutinize me from every angle—circling me like a hyena, even getting up on tiptoe. Meanwhile, all the little kids continued to stare at us. *Sorry, little alien, but you couldn't be inconspicuous if you tried.*

She scattered particles with every step, like a river of stars or the tail of a comet. Then she stopped directly in front of me...and smiled widely, innocently, flashing her pearly whites.

"You know, I must say...ho ho...something about you feels like *destiny*."

"Oh really," I replied offhandedly.

From her looks alone, Yashiro seemed more than capable of affecting a destiny or two. Me, though? As far as I knew, I was just an ordinary teenage girl. Granted, whenever I bleached my hair, my sister shouted "Bad student! Bad student!" and my mom called me a *gyaru*, though I wasn't sure if that was supposed to be an insult or what. But yeah, other than that, I was really pretty normal.

"I think perhaps you were born to meet me."

I certainly hadn't expected anyone to drop that line on me. As I reeled from the impact, I ruminated for a moment, then ultimately asked, "Isn't it supposed to be the other way around?"

Even the other way around, the statement still didn't make sense coming from what appeared to be a small child.

"No, no. I was born to carry out a *multitude* of other tasks," she replied, unsmiling. Apparently, the implication was that *I* had nothing better to do.

This pissed me off, so I pinched her cheeks with both hands and tugged.

"Heh heh heh... You're only wasting your time," she smirked as I squished her face in every direction. She didn't even bat a lash when I puffed her cheeks out like a

176

squirrel. Then I spotted a lock of her butterfly hair poking up from the back of her head and gave that a tug instead.

"Gyaaahhh!"

Super-effective—no squishy cheeks to save her this time.

Once I'd had my fun, I let her go. I looked down at my hands, where a smattering of tiny particles danced in my palm. This time, my first reaction wasn't *What the heck?* but *Wow, pretty.*

"Oh dear. I forgot I was on my way to acquire my dinner for tonight," Yashiro mused, gazing up at the sky as though checking the time. I wasn't sure how she gauged the sun's position through the sheet of clouds, but okay.

Also, "acquire" her dinner? *I'm starting to worry about this kid. But she's probably not sleeping on the street, since she looks like she took a shower today.*

"I imagine we will meet again. Until then, ta-ta and talk to you later." With a curt wave, Yashiro dashed off down the street, the wings of her butterfly hair flapping with her movements, scattering a trail of particles in her wake. Watching her, I found myself mesmerized. She reminded me of that one fairy, Tinkle-bell or whatever her name was. Except less dainty and more food-obsessed.

Every last detail about Yashiro was a mystery, to the point that it was hard to believe we were residents of the same town.

"Now then, where was I…?"

Right—on my way to Adachi's.

I was trying to cast my line in Adachi's direction, but somehow, it felt as though I'd reeled in something entirely different along the way.

The rest of the walk was mostly uneventful. Once I arrived outside Adachi's house, I took out my phone to check my notifications one last time. Nothing. *All right, here we go.* I rang the doorbell. Next, I considered using the intercom to let her know that it was me, but then I heard the bolt unlock. The door swung open.

"Who is it…?" Adachi asked in a dull, sleepy voice, rubbing her eyes. *Girl, you need to check who it is BEFORE you open the door.*

"Hey," I replied, raising my hand in greeting. She froze.

Judging from her messy, unbrushed hair and the ratty old T-shirt she wore, I'd caught her in the middle of a nap. *God, I wish that was me.*

Her eyes widened and widened—and then, without another word, she closed the door just as quickly as she'd opened it, like a video on rewind.

"Hey! Wait!"

"Give me fifteen minutes!"

"What? That's way too long!"

On the other side of the door, I heard the *thump, thump, thump* of footsteps racing down a hallway.

You're seriously going to make me wait out here for fifteen whole minutes? What if your neighbors think I'm casing the joint? I glanced around at the other houses.

"Help! Open up!" I shouted jokingly, pounding on the door. No answer. Defeated, I pressed my back against the door and slid down into a crouch. With nothing else to do, I took out my phone and discovered that it was already past 4:00. As I'd suspected, walking to Adachi's house took quite a long time, especially taking into account a certain glittery alien distraction.

I checked my hands, but the particles had long since faded away. Apparently, the magic wasn't contagious. At first I thought, *Man, if only I could sparkle like that, maybe I wouldn't need to wear makeup.* But then it occurred to me that not everything was *meant* to sparkle. Sure, it looked nice on something inherently beautiful, but on something like...I don't know, a bag of rancid garbage... those same sparkles wouldn't really help much. Not to compare myself to a bag of rancid garbage, obviously.

What exactly was Adachi going to spend those fifteen minutes doing, anyway? Changing out of her pajamas and brushing her hair? Surely she didn't need to dress up fancy just to have a conversation with me. Then again, I understood her not wanting someone she knew to see her looking like a total mess, lest they never look at her the same way again.

To kill time, I alternated between single-player rock-paper-scissors and single-player tic-tac-toe. Really fun, as you can imagine. A while later, the door pressed against my back, so I jumped to my feet and stepped away. This time the door opened slowly, timidly, as Adachi peeked out through the gap.

Her breathing was labored—as though she'd dashed around the house at the speed of light—and her newly-brushed hair was messy again. It seemed to me that it would've been more efficient for Adachi to have me wait longer, or not at all, rather than forcing herself to rush. Furthermore, there was now a new mystery at hand.

"Why'd you put on your uniform?"

"Uh...force of habit," she replied awkwardly, running a hand through her hair. Her flushed cheeks reminded me of what had happened yesterday.

"I hate to break it to you, but you're a little late for school." With this, I finally got a slight smile out of her.

"Oh, shut up." She pushed the door open further, then lowered her hand back to her side, grinning sheepishly. "Man, you can't just randomly show up at my house! You almost gave me a heart attack."

"It wasn't random. I emailed you in advance, didn't I?"

"Did you?"

"Oh my god, you seriously haven't checked your inbox? You dork!" I gave her a playful smack over the head.

She glanced around nervously. "Well... I kinda left my bag in your room."

"*Ohhh*, that explains it!" In other words, her lonely little phone had been beeping to itself in an empty room the whole time.

"Yeah. I figured, you know, I could go without checking it for a day or so, since I don't get a lot of emails," she shrugged. Then, suddenly, her eyes flew open as a lightbulb clicked on in her mind. She took a hasty step forward, slamming her knee into the door. "Did you look around in there?"

"Dude, I forgot your bag was even in my room until literally just now."

"Oh. Okay." She heaved a sigh of relief. Exactly how much private stuff did she keep in there? Now I was starting to get curious.

"Wait a minute... Oh, that explains it! Is *that* why you stayed home today? Because you didn't have your bag?"

"No, I was just sleeping...but it was kinda, maybe, a tiny bit your fault."

Wait, really? I glanced at her. She seemed to realize something, and averted her gaze. Her ears looked ever-so-faintly pink.

"I'm sorry. I should've thought to bring it to you."

"Oh, no, that's okay. I'll be at school tomorrow, so just bring it then."

"All right, will do. And don't worry. I won't try to read your diary or whatever!"

I laughed at my own unfunny joke. Adachi didn't.

"You better not," she insisted sharply, her expression dead serious.

"I won't."

"What did you email me about, anyway?"

"Oh, you know, just 'How's it going, friendo?'"

"Okay, well... I'm doing just peachy, friendo!" She raised her arm and flexed her bicep...then quickly got too embarrassed and had to stop.

I pointed my phone camera at her. "Do it again!"

"No!"

Darn. "So, can I come in, or are we going to stand in the doorway the whole time?"

"Oh, um...actually, I have work today," she explained sadly. Apparently, she was fine with skipping school, but not work.

How very responsible of you...kinda. "Hmm...well, okay. Guess I'll go home." After all, I'd already accomplished what I came here for: saw her, talked to her, cleared up the email thing. Yep, I was basically done.

But, right as I turned to go, Adachi asked, "Wait, what? You're leaving?"

I blinked at her, wondering, *Don't you have to go to work or whatever?*

"I mean, we could talk for a few minutes," she explained quickly.

"Hmm...what would we talk about, though?"

At times like these, we always defaulted to sitting around in silence. We didn't have any hobbies in common—more specifically, I didn't have any hobbies *at all*—and neither of us attended school regularly enough to vent about class.

"Go on, Adachi. Start a conversation."

She was the one who'd told me to stay, so in my opinion, it was *her* responsibility to get the ball rolling. Her face froze in a stiff smile while her eyes screamed, "Oh god, help me!"

"Uhh...how's it going, friendo?"

"Just peachy, friendo."

But I didn't flex my bicep. Instead of returning her serve, I caught the ball and put it in my pocket.

Silence.

Ultimately, I was forced to think of a topic myself.

"So...I guess you slept in today, huh?" I asked, pointing at her now-nonexistent bedhead.

She averted her gaze. "It just kinda happened."

"It just happened, huh? Lucky you. I had to force myself to stay awake all through class."

Seriously, I had been so drowsy, it sounded as though everyone was speaking a foreign language—and not just in English class, either. By this point, I was *really* lagging behind...and I'd need more than just a few minutes of studying each night to catch up.

"So, are you over your cold now?" I teased.

She started fake-coughing. "It gets worse every time someone asks me about it. Must be a really bad strain."

"Yikes! Well, I'm sure you'd feel just *awful* if I caught it from you, so I'd better go!"

"Noooo! I'm joking! I'm over it!"

Wait, so she did *have a cold?*

As we grinned at each other, the conversation slowly died again. Normally that was totally fine, but today, for some reason, we were obliged to keep talking at any cost.

"Come on, Adachi. Next topic," I said, prompting her with a "let's-hear-it" hand gesture. She opened her mouth to speak, and I noticed her eyes dart back and forth nervously.

"Say, uh, Shimamura?"

"Hmm?" I wasn't expecting her to actually think of anything to say, so I was kind of curious.

She hesitated, and then asked, "Would you want to go on a dat—day trip with me somewhere? Like, on Saturday or something?"

"Day trip? Like where?" I asked. I could think of a dozen more questions, too.

"Uhh...anywhere?" Adachi mumbled.

"You don't have work on Saturday?"

"Not till late, so I could hang out during the day."

"Okay, well... Sure, I don't mind. But *you* have to decide where we're going. I hate planning stuff."

"Okay," she replied, nodding. A smile crept onto her face.

"Okay, cool... Well, I'd better go now. Have fun at work."

Only a few minutes had passed since I'd last tried to leave, but we were well and truly out of topics. This time, however, Adachi let me go without complaint; she seemed satisfied, I guess. Her hand was already reaching for the doorknob.

The day trip would be my first time hanging out with Adachi on a weekend. Then again, perhaps today counted as a weekend, too. For her, anyway. Heh.

"Oh yeah—where'd you get that cool shirt you were wearing? The one with the elephant?"

"Shut up!"

With that parting comment, I walked out to the street and headed on my way.

Five minutes later, I found myself murmuring aloud, "Was I hearing things, or..."

...Did she almost say "go on a date with me"?

Nah, couldn't be.

We agreed to meet up inside a huge shopping mall, in an area with benches and a giant tree. I suggested meeting outside Shimamura Co. for maximum irony, but Adachi didn't really laugh. *Never mind, then.*

When I got there, a group of six elderly men were sitting on the benches, relaxing and sipping cups of coffee as though they lived here. Idly, I wondered what they were up to that day. Then I overheard parts of their conversation and learned that they were headed to the on-site bowling alley afterward. I'd gone there one time with my little sister, back when they first opened. From what I remembered, the place had pool tables and darts and all kinds of cool stuff.

As I reminisced, I snuck another glance to my left. Sure enough, *she* was still there.

"What are *you* doing here?" I finally asked.

"Oh! Destiny!" Yashiro exclaimed. The way she said it made it sound like Destiny was my name or something.

Yes, you read correctly. Inexplicably, Yashiro was at the meetup spot. In fact, when she spotted me, she walked right up and plopped down next to me on the bench. She wasn't wearing her space suit or helmet, but she sat with her arms folded for some reason.

"Neither of us knew the other would be here today, and yet we found each other regardless. Surely it must be destiny." She snickered to herself, puffing her cheeks out.

There you go, tossing that word around again. "Where do you get your lines from? You know, your...dialogue?"

"Extensive study of the media known as 'television shows.'"

"I knew it. All this 'destiny' talk sounded *way* too dramatic to be real."

Looking at her little baby face, I got the distinct feeling she had *no idea* what "destiny" really meant.

She once again wore her hair in that same butterfly style, but this time, it didn't look quite so tight. Clearly, she was at least capable of learning from her mistakes. Her clothes were different, too; she was wearing a blue skirt paired with a shirt that read *FLAT BUTTE* on the front.

"What are you, a tourist?"

"No, I'm an alien. From the future."

She puffed out her chest, emphasizing her *FLAT BUTTE*. The more I looked at the shirt, the more impressed I became. Believe it or not, Flat Butte was the name of a real, actual place, which meant the people who lived there had to write "Flat Butte" on their envelopes whenever they sent a letter. They probably thought nothing of it. *It's amazing what people can grow accustomed to over time. It's only been five minutes, and I'm already getting over it.*

"So, what brings you here today?" Yashiro asked.

"Hah! I'd like to ask you the same thing. Anyway, I'm meeting a friend."

"Oh *ho*." She nodded as though she didn't know what else to say. I wasn't sure that she was even listening to me.

"What about you?"

"I just came here on a whim. Spotted you purely by chance."

"Oh really?"

"Destiny, wouldn't you say?"

"Yeah, yeah, whatever," I shrugged.

Then Adachi turned up. This mall was quite a distance from her house, so I was expecting her to take the bus, but she slumped forward, hands on her knees, clearly out of breath. Apparently, she'd biked here. After a few seconds, she looked up at me and smiled.

But then she noticed who I was sitting next to, and her face froze.

"I saw you two together the other day, correct? Greetings." Yashiro bowed deeply.

Gee, how polite of you. Just try not to get your glitter everywhere.

"Uh, what? Who are you?" Adachi blinked, baffled. No surprise there. I imagined that she was confused for a myriad of reasons.

"Go get your you-know-what," I told Yashiro.

"Ah! Just a moment."

Clearly, Yashiro knew exactly what I meant by this, because she dashed off around the corner. When she returned, she was wearing her helmet again, just like last time. *How does she do that?* I wondered. I decided to stop thinking about it before I fried my brain.

"See?" I said to Adachi. "It's the little space alien from last time."

"It's me!" Yashiro shouted through the helmet, cheerfully raising both arms into the air. But she was starting to look creepy with the helmet on, so I pulled it off again. If I could touch it, which I could, and it had weight, which it did, then it couldn't have been a mere illusion.

"Hmm."

Curious, I put it on. Instantly, everything went pitch black except for the visor directly in front of my eyes. Not only was the helmet really heavy, it was also extremely hard to breathe in.

I turned to Adachi. "How do I look?"

She hastily took a step backward. "Like a worse version of Shimamura."

She snatched the helmet off my head, then looked at me as though she didn't know what she was supposed to do with it. Apparently, she didn't want to try it on. I flicked my gaze at Yashiro, as if to say, "Well, give it back, then." Timidly, Adachi held the helmet in Yashiro's direction.

Yashiro took it and tucked it under her arm. "What is your name?"

Adachi's lips moved hesitantly. "Uh...A-Adachi. And...who are you?" She looked from Yashiro to me, her eyes silently asking me to explain our relationship.

To me, Yashiro was...an acquaintance, I guess? I couldn't really call her a friend.

"Put simply," said Yashiro, "I am an alien from the future."

"Translation...?" Adachi asked me.

"Eh, just think of her as the local weird kid," I shrugged.

I didn't know Yashiro's real identity, and I wasn't ditzy enough to accept her little "story" at face value. But, at the same time, I'd have to be a blind idiot to ignore the fact that she *radiated blue sparkles*. As in, literally right at that moment. They floated in the air around her like phosphorus.

The only thing I knew for sure about Yashiro was that she liked sweets...and *me,* for some reason, although I'd barely spoken to her and definitely hadn't done anything to earn her affection. Or was it because I gave her that donut?

Sadly, while Yashiro might have sensed "destiny" between us, the feeling wasn't mutual. Why would it have been? She was an astronaut on the outside and a little fairy freak on the inside. It was kind of a lot, if that makes sense.

"Is this the friend you were waiting for?" Yashiro asked, pointing to Adachi.

"Yeah."

"Then let's be on our way."

She started walking.

"What?"

I stared after her. She turned back.

"It's time I repaid you for the donut you gave me. I shall treat you to a meal."

Adachi shot me a look like, "She's coming with us?"

I turned back to Yashiro. "You're coming with us?"

"I smell something delicious in that direction," she announced, completely ignoring me. Seriously, she was so self-centered, she gave my sister a run for her money.

Adachi furrowed her brow. "What's going on?"

Apparently, this turn of events had thrown her for a loop. Well, she wasn't the only one. All I knew for certain was that Adachi was *not* happy about it.

Meanwhile, Yashiro was now several steps away. She turned back again, beckoning us. "You'd better hurry and catch up before you get lost!"

If anyone's going to get lost in here, it's you, I thought, but shrugged it off and started walking. Then I remembered something, and grabbed Adachi by the wrist. She flinched as though I'd zapped her with a jolt of electricity, then looked at me with eyes as wide as saucers. Evidently, she hadn't expected me to do that.

"Wh-what?"

"Oh, I just don't want you running away this time."

"Huh? Oh…"

She seemed to realize what I was referring to: the day we'd hung out at the station square. Once again, it was me, her, and Yashiro.

Adachi looked away awkwardly, but I pretended I didn't see it. Instead, I smiled. "It'd be a real shame if you came all this way only to turn around and leave again."

If she went home now, what would I even do with the rest of my afternoon?

Adachi rubbed her cheek, her expression still dismal. Maybe she had an itch or something.

"I'm not gonna run away, but..."

"I know you're not happy about this. I'm not exactly excited myself. But for now, let's just humor her."

Dragging Adachi along, I made a beeline for Yashiro. I couldn't think of any real reason why I shouldn't let her treat us to a meal, after all. If anything, I was surprised she had the money for it.

"Oh yeah, and good morning," I said to Adachi as we walked.

She wasn't sure how to process that at first. She blinked once, twice, then smiled vaguely. "Morning," she replied. At last, she started walking with us of her own volition.

And so, the two of us followed the little blue fairy. With her bright sparkles serving as a beacon to guide us,

I couldn't help but wonder if we were on our way to a fairytale world.

In the end, Yashiro led us to a restaurant right next to the on-site grocery store. Judging from the sign, the place served pizza, pasta, and an omelet soufflé dish. The restaurant was a surprisingly competent choice, actually. *I bet if Yashiro knew there was a donut shop near the entrance, she'd turn around and run all the way there.*

"Yes, good!"

Drawn in by the scrumptious scent, Yashiro staggered headfirst into the restaurant. Naturally, the hostess was somewhat startled to encounter a little fairy-looking girl, but she quickly recovered and greeted Yashiro with a smile.

"Table for three," Yashiro announced before the hostess could get a word in.

Inside, the restaurant clientele was predominantly middle-aged women. The hostess seated us at a booth between two full tables.

Yashiro slid in first; naturally, my gaze shifted to the opposite side of the table. But before I could sit down, Yashiro waved me over.

"Come, join me!"

"Huh? Oh, okay."

At her prompting, I slid in next to her. Her little grin was so cute and innocent, I reached out and stroked her hair purely on instinct, as though she were my sister or something. Blue sparkles spilled out from under my palm.

As I sat, my other hand brushed against Adachi's wrist. I realized I was still holding onto her like a vise, preventing her from sitting down.

"Ack! Sorry!"

I hastily let go. Surely, she wouldn't run out of the restaurant, right? She'd told me she wouldn't, anyway. But Adachi didn't move; she looked at Yashiro with a pout on her lips, like a grumpy little kid. Then she pushed lightly against my shoulder. "Scoot in, Shimamura."

"Huh? Oh, okay." *I sound like a broken record.*

Once I did as requested, Adachi sat down next to me.

"Wait, what...?"

Why would we all sit on the same side? It's not like we're waiting for more people to join us! Even the hostess looked a little confused as she set a glass of water down in front of each of us.

Stuck in the middle, it would be kind of a hassle for me to try to move to the other side...but Adachi seemingly had no intention of moving, either. She kept shooting me awkward, furtive glances. *Oh, you think this is awkward for you? Try being me!*

Meanwhile, Yashiro downed her water as though everything was perfectly normal.

"Okay, well... Let me know when you're ready to order," said the hostess. She set a menu down on the table and hurried away. Clearly, she sensed the weirdness between the three of us.

Some people were gifted with almost supernatural intuition. *Maybe, through evolution, we'll be able to see ghosts someday.* This was decidedly not the sort of thing that should have occupied my mind at a restaurant.

Yashiro set her empty glass down onto the table and pointed at an item near the top of the menu. "I've already decided that I'm going to have this wonderful, fluffy omelet soufflé," she announced. In the photo, a miniature griddle cradled a perfectly browned rolled omelet.

It looked really good. I was tempted to order it for myself, but then I glanced around at the other tables and saw their brightly colored pizzas. *I could go for that, too. Or the pasta.* In other words, I was hungry for basically the entire menu.

"What are you getting, Adachi?"

"You can order whatever you like," Yashiro added with a smug grin.

Adachi glanced at us, then reached for the menu.

"Can I grab that real quick? It's hard to see from here."

"Sure thing."

I handed the menu to her. She unfolded it and held it up around herself like a shield, preventing anyone else from reading it. Not that Yashiro needed to, of course. She'd already decided, and now she was kicking her legs back and forth under the table like a little kid on a sugar high.

Adachi tugged my sleeve. "What are you getting, Shimamura?"

At her prompting, I leaned in close to look at the menu with her. "Hmm...not sure."

I watched as a pizza arrived for a table near us. It was *way* too much for a single person to eat by themselves.

"What if we ordered a pizza and a pasta dish and went halfsies?" I suggested.

"Sure." Adachi nodded cheerfully.

Just then, Yashiro poked my side. I yelped and whirled around to find her prodding me all over.

"Hey!" I reached out and pinched her cheeks. "What's the big idea, missy?"

Yashiro let out a muffled giggle through her contorted lips. "I was bored," she declared.

"Oh, I see. So, whenever you get bored, you violate people's personal space?"

Apparently, she's a lot more dangerous than she looks. I squished and stretched her face in all different directions to idle away the time.

Suddenly, I felt Adachi grab my *other* side, and I let out a second yelp. *What is it with you people and touching my sides? I'm not a huge fan of it!*

With my hands still grasping Yashiro's face, I turned in Adachi's direction. She glared down at the menu. *Seriously, just use your words and tell me what you want from me.*

"You choose the pizza, and I'll choose the pasta," Adachi suggested offhandedly, still grasping my shirt.

"Pffggehh," Yashiro whimpered. She, likewise, was still trapped in my grasp.

Ugh, whatever. I don't care. "Okay, I choose this one." It was the bacon-zucchini pizza.

"Cool, then I'll get this," Adachi replied, pointing at the sun-ripened tomato pasta.

With our orders decided, we flagged down the hostess. She walked up with a barely suppressed smile on her face, almost as though she was biting back a laugh. Probably because I was squishing Yashiro's cheeks, although I doubted that Yashiro and I looked remotely like siblings.

Adachi ordered for us, since she was nearest to the hostess. In sharp contrast to Yashiro and I, her voice was flat and emotionless; it caught me by surprise, and I relinquished my grip on Yashiro, who let out a sigh of relief and rubbed her cheeks.

"You can order more than that, you know," she added a moment later, once she regained her usual swagger. Adachi met this with a dry laugh.

Once the hostess left with our orders, there was a long silence. Yashiro folded her paper napkin into some sort of origami while Adachi and I just sat there as usual.

Actually, it felt like Adachi was in a bad mood for some reason. Did she have some kind of problem with Yashiro? If so, what was it about the girl that Adachi didn't like?

I glanced over at Yashiro.

She stood out in sharp contrast against the white walls behind her. In motion or at rest, something about her *commanded* attention. With her oddly colored hair and perfect, symmetrical face, she seemed like the kind of person who could change the world—like a superhero capable of piloting a giant mech or something. But in reality...

"Heh heh heh. It's a grasshopper. What do you think?" she asked with a smirk.

I think it looks more like a chopstick rest. Even I could do better than that. I grabbed a napkin and started folding.

"What is that, a chopstick rest?"

"It's a grasshopper, exactly like yours."

"But that looks nothing like mine." She frowned, tilting her head in innocent confusion. *God, she pisses me off.*

"Whose origami looks more like a grasshopper? Mine, right?" I asked Adachi. She sat with her elbow on the table and her chin in her hand, looking annoyed for some reason. She glanced at me.

"*Neither* of them look like a grasshopper," she replied. *Grrr, you're no fun.*

"You Earthlings are completely blind, aren't you? Poor things," the obnoxious alien lamented behind me. I ignored her.

"Adachi!"

I put my hand on Adachi's shoulder to draw her attention—and, as soon as she turned to look, I grabbed her by the cheeks. She didn't expect it at all, so I pulled it off on the first try. Initially, her face froze, but then blood steadily rushed to her head, and her cheeks burned pink.

"What's up, buttercup?" I asked, cupping her face in my hands and forcing her to look at me. Against my palms, I felt her bad mood seemingly fade as confusion settled in instead. I gave her cheeks a squish, and her whole expression softened, even her eyes.

"Nnn...nuffinghphh."

"Okay then, let's hear your favorite catchphrase. And don't forget to smile."

"*What*? What catchphrase?"

"You remember, don't you? First I start by asking, 'How's it going, friendo?' Now it's your turn!"

At this, Adachi put two and two together. "Ugh, c'mon," she growled, looking away. But in the end she relented, donning the best smile she could manage through squished cheeks, her gaze still averted.

"Doing just peachy, friendo."

She even remembered to flex her bicep, but this time, she dropped the pose just as quickly as she struck it. I wasn't complaining, though.

It occurred to me that Yashiro had been quiet for quite some time. When I turned to check on her, I found her in the middle of crafting her second grasshopper, while her first sat side by side with mine. Did she plan to make a little tabletop grasshopper kingdom or what? *Eh, she's not hurting anybody, I guess.*

I decided to leave Yashiro to her own devices; I let go of Adachi while I was at it. Adachi reached up to clutch her head, possibly out of embarrassment, so I went ahead and told her what was on my mind.

"Look... I'm not a mind reader, but now that we're here, we should at least *try* to have fun, don't you think?"

I felt Adachi peek at me through her fingers. She didn't respond verbally, but I saw her nod slightly. Feeling weirdly satisfied, I continued to twiddle my thumbs and wait for our food to arrive.

"Oh, it's coming! Hey, over here!" Yashiro shouted, waving her hands at the hostess like a lunatic. I cringed internally. It wasn't like I could chastise her for drawing attention to herself when her outward appearance already did that in spades.

The hostess set down a miniature griddle in front of Yashiro. Unlike the menu picture, however, the omelet on the griddle wasn't very puffy at all. Yashiro looked at it for a moment, then reached out and dumped an unreasonable amount of maple syrup all over it.

"Sploosh!"

Without so much as a glance at the tomato sauce that came with the omelet, she stabbed her fork into the dish and took a bite. Inside the omelet, I saw what looked like pieces of French bread mixed into the egg... Admittedly, I was curious to try it.

"Oh, it's so moist! Wow! Very moist!" Yashiro exclaimed as she continued to cut up her omelet.

Yes, yes, we heard you the first time. Considering the amount of syrup she'd poured onto the dish, I wouldn't have expected anything else. I found myself staring at it, wondering how much syrup had seeped in.

Next, she moved on to the soufflé, which she ate with such gusto that it piqued my interest even further. Once she'd swallowed her current mouthful, I spoke up.

"Can I get a bite of that?"

"Certainly." She cut off a chunk and scooped it onto her fork. "Here."

"Wha...?!" Adachi exclaimed, before I even had time to react. I turned to find her visibly scandalized.

"What's the matter? Did you want some?"

"Not really." She shifted her gaze, and I sensed that she had more to say, but then I caught her glancing furtively at Yashiro's fork. *She totally wants a bite, I just know it. Wait... But then, why didn't she speak up when I first asked?*

"Hurry it along, lass," Yashiro urged.

"Yeah, yeah... Wait, what's with the accent all of a sudden?" *Now you're a* Scottish *time-traveling alien?* I turned back to her. "Oh, no, I don't want that part. I want the part with French bread."

"Very demanding, aren't we, Shimamura-san?"

"Yeah, I get that a lot."

Yashiro put the current forkful into her own mouth, then scooped up another piece in line with my request and brought it right to my lips. I bent forward slightly and took the bite into my mouth.

Instantly, before I even started chewing, overwhelming sweetness seeped into my gums. It felt as though my teeth were all going to fall out simultaneously. There wasn't much depth to the flavor, either—just *sweet, sweet, sweet*. It was hard to tell whether I actually liked it or not.

"Gah! Sugar overload! I think you put *way* too much maple syrup on."

"Too much...?" She frowned slightly, as if to suggest it wasn't nearly enough.

Good grief. I smiled at her. Just then, something touched my side again, and I felt another tug on my shirt. This time, Adachi had seized not just the fabric, but my body along with it.

"You know, Adachi, it's not nice to grab somebody's love handles like that."

"Right, sorry. Here, you can have a bite of this."

Where did that *come from?* I turned to find that Adachi's pasta had arrived.

"Wait... Weren't we going halfsies on this anyway?"

"Yeah, but...um...I'll give you an extra bite for free."

She hastily twirled a strand of pasta onto her fork and held it to my mouth. *You're not trying to fatten me up, are you?* For a moment I hesitated, but ultimately decided that it would be rude to reject her kind offer, so I put her fork in my mouth. The taste of tomato and olive oil danced across my tongue.

Yashiro with her sweet dish versus Adachi with savory. Somehow the flavors seemed to match them perfectly.

As I savored my bite of pasta, Adachi stared at Yashiro, whose entire chin was now sticky with sauce. Yashiro was so focused on eating, she didn't notice Adachi watching her. Adachi didn't seem actively hostile toward Yashiro, but she did strike me as recalcitrant, like a little kid with her new stepmother. Yeah, she could be really immature sometimes.

After I returned the fork to Adachi, she stared down at it, then shook her head. *Seriously, what's going on with her?*

It was exhausting, having to play mediator between these two. If one of them asked me, "Where to after this?" my response would be, "The pharmacy," because I probably had an ulcer by now. As one might imagine, that made for a less-than-enjoyable mealtime experience.

When I asked myself how we'd gotten here, I knew that deep down, I had an inkling. Instead of actually examining it, though, I dodged the question and looked in the direction of the kitchen. *Where's that pizza?* A pleasant, slightly burnt smell wafted from the kiln.

However, this day was far from over, and things were about to get a whole lot worse for the three of us.

That's what Destiny was telling me, anyway.

I once read somewhere that a bowling ball weighs the same as a human head. No idea whether that's true, but it would certainly explain where neck pain comes from.

"This item is heavy," Yashiro complained as she held her ball in both hands.

She stumbled in my direction—I wasn't about to let her drop that thing on my foot, so I took a hasty step back. Unfortunately, she followed me.

"A skillful move. Truly the work of destiny."

Why is it always about destiny with you?

After we finished eating, we figured it'd be a waste to go straight home. Adachi and I debated window shopping, but then a certain alien child spotted the on-site amusement center and started babbling excitedly. Since Adachi and I were both generally passive in social situations, we found ourselves dragged along.

Mind you, the facility had a lot more to offer than just bowling—karaoke, billiards, darts, and ping-pong too. Naturally I suggested ping-pong, since it was kind of our thing, but we quickly realized that'd get complicated with an odd number of players.

A bunch of creepy older guys were hogging the darts area, and Yashiro wasn't tall enough to lean over the pool table. Thus, through the process of elimination, we ended up at the bowling alley—690 yen per game. Yashiro didn't want to foot the bill this time, so we split it between us instead.

Adachi paid her share without complaint, but she hadn't joined the conversation in quite a while. Every now and then, I felt her gaze on me and turned to look, only for her to shake her head and say "It's nothing." *You sure about that?*

Honestly, perhaps it was for the best that Yashiro took charge. Who knew what Adachi and I would have ended up doing otherwise.

"So, what do I do with this?" Yashiro asked me, still cradling her blue bowling ball.

"You don't know how to play? But *you're* the one who wanted to go bowling!"

"I can always tell when something will be entertaining. Impressive, right?"

"Not really." I grabbed her by the head and turned her to face the lanes. "See those pins? You roll the ball and try to knock them down."

On the back wall, above the pins, hung a large monitor that displayed feeds of all the lanes. Precisely at that moment, a guy from the family next to us (the dad, I assume) was taking his turn, so I adjusted Yashiro's view accordingly. He wore what looked like pro bowling gloves, but it quickly became apparent that his skill level was anything but "pro."

Early into his throw, the ball deviated from the center and careened toward the gutter. Luckily for him, the family was playing with bumpers, so the ball bounced back toward the middle and slowly took down pin after pin. In the end, the throw was deemed a strike, and the dad jumped for joy.

"So, yeah, that's the gist of it. Got it?"

"Tricked you! I actually *knew* how to play the whole time. Ha ha! You fell for my ninjutsu!"

I gave her a little smack on the cheek to set her straight. The impact scattered light particles everywhere. They floated toward my hand, which startled me so badly I nearly fell backward. It seemed as though each particle had a mind of its own. *What* are *you, Yashiro?*

Nevertheless, she remained at my side like a faithful puppy, speaking only to me and never to Adachi. As for

Adachi, she willingly interacted with me, but obviously she had zero intention of playing nice with Yashiro.

I know I can't expect you to be best friends, but have either of you thought about what it feels like for me? To be stuck in the middle like this? I was by no means a talkative person, and I was dying for something to drink.

After watching the family next to us for a moment, Yashiro turned back to me. "Shimamura-san!" she called gleefully. "Can I go first?!"

She tried to lift her bowling ball and staggered again. *I'm really starting to worry about you.* "Sure, why not?"

"Heh heh heh... I have a brilliant plan." From the way her eyes gleamed, I could tell she was up to no good.

Then I noticed Adachi intently staring off in a different direction, so I decided to approach her. "You better not run away," I warned her—in a playful way, of course, not a mean way.

"I told you, I won't," she replied, pouting like a little kid. Then her expression softened slightly. "You're a total mom friend, aren't you, Shimamura?"

"I've tolerated my kid sister for half my life, so...I guess you could say I know how to deal with little goblins."

"So, this girl's like a second sister? What about me?"

"You can call me Oneechan if you want," I joked,

expecting Adachi to laugh and shoot me down. Instead there was a pause, and then... *Wait, are you—*

"...Oneechan."

Oh god, she went there. And with a straight face. And what was that awkward pause?

"Wh-what's up, my sweet little sister?" I asked, playing along, although deep down I wasn't really looking to adopt any more goblins.

Just then, Adachi looked up. The blood drained from her face.

"Uh, Shimamura?"

She pointed over at the lanes. Curious, I turned...and saw Yashiro, ball in hand, walking down our assigned lane as though it were the most natural thing in the world. *Wait, where are your shoes?!* Everyone stared at her. I heard whispers from the other bowlers around us.

Obviously I couldn't just let her cause a scene, so I dashed over to stop her, sighing internally. *What am I, her babysitter?* Once I caught up, I grabbed her by the scruff of the neck.

"Hm?" She turned to face me, puzzled. But I wanted answers.

"Excuse me, little missy! What the heck do you think you're doing?"

"As I observed the other players, I realized that there's a distinct disadvantage to throwing the ball from a distance."

"*What*?"

"From up close, however, anyone can easily knock down all the pins! Don't you see?" She smirked at me as she explained her *brilliant plan*. Listening to her nearly sapped me of the will to live.

"Wow. You're so smart."

"I know, right?"

"*But,* unfortunately for you, this is a bowling alley, so you're going to have to play by the rules." I dragged her back down the lane, away from the pins. *If you want to put your own spin on bowling, go do that at home.*

"Noooo! It's not fair!"

"*You're* the one not playing fair. Now stand at the end of the lane, and roll the ball like you're supposed to."

She cocked her head at me.

"Do you seriously not know how to play...?"

"We don't have this game back on my home planet," she replied offhandedly. It didn't appear to be an act, either. Was she raised in some remote foreign country? If so, then her Japanese was *ridiculously* good for a non-native speaker. She was a walking mystery I couldn't begin to solve.

"What's the deal with your hair, anyway? That's your natural color?" I asked finally.

Yashiro grabbed a handful of her own hair. "What, this?"

"Yes, *that*. Last I checked, nobody on Earth has naturally blue hair."

"Stylish, isn't it?"

"I was thinking *bizarre*, but sure."

"I intended to model myself after my compatriot, you see, but I inadvertently chose the girl next to her instead."

What are you talking *about?* I attempted to translate Yashiro's make-believe into reality. Maybe she had wanted the same hairstyle as one of her...relatives? But she found herself mimicking their friend? No, that didn't make sense...unless her relative had a blue-haired friend, in which case that person was almost certainly an alien. And in *that* case...what did that make Yashiro?

"Meh...I guess I shouldn't think about it too hard. All right, let's see you do a normal throw this time." I gave her a little push.

"Very well, if you insist." She toddled up to the start of the lane. *Finally, a return to normalcy,* I thought.

Oh, how wrong I was.

Yashiro launched into a full-body dive and released the ball while sliding on her stomach. Her form was so sloppy, it almost looked as though she'd simply tripped at the starting line. I'd never seen anyone bowl like that in my entire life. Still, I imagined it was fun to watch the ball roll down the lane from that angle.

The ball crashed into the bumper and bounced off, flying directly into the pins and mowing them all down at the speed of light. A perfect strike.

Naturally, Yashiro's abnormal throw style garnered even more attention from the rest of the alley, but she didn't move a muscle. I walked over, put my hands under her tummy, and hoisted her up. She turned to look at me. "Was that good?"

"Uh...sure, I guess, but what the heck was that dive?"

"I figured it would be advantageous to get as close as possible."

"On second thought...maybe your blue hair is the least of my concerns." *If Nagafuji tried the same stunt, I bet it'd be painful. For her boobs, I mean.*

Sliding on the ground had gotten the front of Yashiro's clothes all dirty, so I dusted her off.

Maybe I am *the mom friend... Isn't this pretty normal, though?*

I headed back to Adachi with the alien cradled in my arms. Her little legs swayed with every step, and I found myself sorely wishing she would walk on her own two feet already. Still, her body was abnormally lightweight, so I couldn't really complain. *Maybe she's made of Styrofoam on the inside. Or maybe her whole body is one big fusion of light particles.* For some stupid reason, I found myself picturing this.

All alien speculation aside, I had a feeling Adachi would be in a bad mood when we returned, and sure enough, she was. I sighed and shook my head. *Man, it's hard work having a "little sister" my own age.*

Once I sat down, Yashiro shifted onto my lap like a dog. She didn't seem to want to move, either. I didn't mind much, since she was so light, but I felt like I was going to choke on all the sparkles.

"Wanna go next, Adachi?"

"No thanks."

"Too bad," I insisted, and handed her the bowling ball sitting ready nearby. By that point, I'd learned that bossiness was the most effective strategy for dealing with Adachi when she threw a tantrum.

Sure enough, her bad attitude faded as she reluctantly took the ball. Evidently, she caved quickly to peer pressure. *Same, TBH.*

"So, is there a point to winning?" Yashiro asked me. She didn't seem to be gloating about her strike, either; her voice was perfectly level. Perhaps she genuinely didn't see the value in victory for victory's sake. When she looked at me with her innocent eyes, I hesitated. I *really* wasn't sure what to tell her.

"I don't know… Doesn't it feel good to outdo everyone else?"

"Not when I'm competing against someone I love. And I love you, Shimamura-san."

At this, my heart nearly stopped. That kind of thing always tended to put me on edge. A split-second later, there was a dull *THUD* as Adachi dropped her bowling ball. I turned and watched as she chased after it. *Such a child.*

"Oh, uh…cool. Thanks."

I kept my gaze averted. As you might expect, it was kind of awkward to make eye contact with somebody who had just professed their love for me. Especially for someone like me. I had notoriously struggled with expressing my feelings since I was a kid.

Once Adachi recovered her ball, she walked back over and stood in front of us—but her gaze was fixed on Yashiro, not me. There was a palpable hostility in the air.

"How about you compete with me?" she demanded, holding her ball aloft. It was hard to tell from her poker face, but I sensed that she was actually upset about something. *Whatsa matter, little Adachi-chan?*

"Oh ho… You think you can beat a pro bowlinger such as myself?"

I'm pretty sure the word you're looking for is "bowler."
Then again, you're also lying through your teeth, so I guess
it's a wash.

"You bet I do," Adachi shot back, lightly stroking her
bowling ball's smooth surface in much the same way a
supervillain would pet their cat. "If I win…"

She immediately stopped short and looked at me.

What? If you win, you want me to do something? I'm
not Yashiro's mom, so you can go ahead and leave me out
of it!

"Let me borrow you for a minute."

Taking Yashiro by the hand, Adachi pulled her down
from my lap and led her to a distant corner of the bowling alley. Holding hands, you'd think they'd come off as
siblings. Instead, their short walk more closely resembled
an attempted kidnapping. Probably because they looked
nothing alike.

Adachi crouched down to Yashiro's eye level and whispered in her ear. The little alien put a hand to her chin in
contemplation.

Once Adachi finished speaking, Yashiro replied,
"Hmmm. No thanks."

Wow, that was blunt.

She bounced all the way back like a little rabbit. I found
myself impressed at how she seemed to exude energy. In

contrast, Adachi trudged back with slumped shoulders, probably because Yashiro had shot her down point-blank.

Adachi took her ball and lobbed it from the end of the lane like a normal person; it took down six pins. On one hand, it was nice to see that at least one of us knew how to bowl correctly, but on the other hand, I wasn't really sure how to react. Should I compliment Adachi or console her?

Silently, she attempted her second throw. In the end, however, she failed to take down the last two pins. Scratching her head, she returned to her seat next to me. Since she was technically losing, I decided to comfort her.

"That was close."

"I don't have a lot of experience with this game," she explained. Since she'd mentioned previously that her relationship with her family wasn't great, I could tell that she wasn't just making excuses for her poor performance. After all, she wasn't the type of person to plan a bowling night with friends. "Anyway, it's your turn, Shimamura."

"Oh, yeah..." I shifted Yashiro to the empty seat on my other side, then reluctantly got to my feet. I'd already paid for the right to play...but I wasn't sure I had any business butting in on their little competition. *Maybe it'd be more considerate to drop out?* I turned around to shoot them an inquiring look.

"Hurry up, Shimamura."

"Oh...uh...okay."

At Adachi's prompting, I decided to just throw the ball and get it over with. *Hyah! There, all done.* I didn't even care how many pins I hit—it didn't matter to me. After all, there were more important things in life than winning or losing.

When I returned to my seat, my little lapdog crawled right back into her usual spot. Apparently, she enjoyed using other people as chairs.

"I beg your pardon? It's *your* turn, remember?"

"Ah, yes, of course."

She jumped down from my lap, and I found myself wondering what had happened to her astronaut helmet. The more I thought about that, the more it threatened to fry my brain.

"Now then, pardon me while the pro bowlinger takes her second turn."

BOWLER, not bowlinger. That sounds like a type of airplane.

As she jogged over to grab her ball, blue sparkles scattered in a stream behind her, drawing the attention of a nearby family and a group of teenage boys. Not that I blamed them for staring, since she immediately followed up with her ridiculous diving-throw technique.

Meanwhile, I wondered if it hurt to bend her neck at that angle.

Her dives didn't cross the foul line, so they were probably valid throws—not that an amateur like me would have known. Once again, the ball sped down the lane at a weird angle, bounced around, and ultimately upheld its end of the bargain, toppling pin after pin until not a single one was left standing.

"Wowie."

Bumper handicap aside, who'd have thought that her insane throw style would net her two strikes in a row? Certainly not me. In fact, I was starting to suspect that she might have some kind of weird alien superpower to go with her weird alien hair. Frankly, it wouldn't have surprised me if she did. *Then again, if she had superpowers, I guess she wouldn't need to do these wacky dive throws.*

"And what a great second turn it was!" Yashiro exclaimed, dashing back to me with both hands outstretched in front of her for some reason. More concerning, however, was the fact that her legs were all pink. Sighing internally, I resigned myself to my mom-friend duties.

"You haven't scraped your knees, have you?"

I reached out and touched them to be sure. Nope, no scrapes. She didn't wince in pain or anything, either. Somehow, touching her little legs made me realize just how *small* she was. The thought that this tiny child had bought me lunch made me low-key hate myself.

Meanwhile, Adachi had a big scowl on her face. No surprise there, of course. At the rate she was going, Yashiro would keep getting strike after strike, which meant Adachi didn't stand a chance.

"Good thing you guys didn't make that bet after all, huh?" It was the most consolation I could offer Adachi at this point. She growled quietly.

"Heh heh heh! You know, you're free to copy me if you like," Yashiro announced with a smug smirk.

Adachi glanced at her, but otherwise said nothing, though she had "Thanks for the unwanted advice" written all over her face.

"Or *you* could just throw the ball like a normal person," I retorted. It was hard to deny the efficacy of Yashiro's dive throw, though, especially since I couldn't be sure whether it was against the rules. *Add it to the pile of other Yashiro mysteries, I guess.*

Adachi got up and grabbed her ball. Personally, I was impressed that she had the courage to keep going.

Holding the ball in front of her face, she walked toward me, gaze averted, and asked, "So, uh, who are you rooting for?"

"Uhhhh..." *Man, don't ask me that. What a pain.*

"Yes, yes, do tell!" Yashiro chimed in cheerfully.

Ugh...I wish you wouldn't make me pick.

At first glance, I might have seemed like a "mom friend" or whatever. However, I was actually as lazy as the next girl. No amount of effort or experience could change that.

Whenever someone came to me for attention, assistance, or affection, some part of me felt...resistant. I was always struck by the urge to shrink myself down as small as possible and slink away quietly.

To everyone else, this was probably *hilarious*. I could imagine they enjoyed tormenting me. No point in chasing without something to chase, after all. Conversely, if I leaned into it and actively *tried* to get their attention, they'd lose all interest. At least, that's how it seemed like to me.

Since I had that attitude toward other people, deep down, I knew I was honestly better off going through life alone...and yet here I was.

"Shimamura-san!"

"Shimamura!"

"Yes, yes, I hear you," I replied quickly.

Somehow, I felt like the main character in a romcom... and I was *exhausted*.

Following this fairly tumultuous day out, I came home to find that it was still only three o'clock. Admittedly, I wasn't expecting to be home quite that early...but after we'd bowled our ten frames, we all sort of awkwardly went our separate ways. (I'll spare you the details of who won and who was a sore loser, but I'm sure you can guess.)

I walked into my room and immediately collapsed onto my futon. "Man, I'm beat." That was the only sentiment I expressed aloud. Truth be told, I wanted nothing more than to fuse with the floor and take a six-hour nap, but for some reason my mind was still wide awake. After about ten minutes of lying there motionlessly, I got bored and opened my eyes.

I spotted a manga volume lying nearby. Apparently, my sister had been reading it before bed last night. I picked it up and opened to a random page, where the protagonist was making excuses about something or other.

"Heh heh heh." With a goofy laugh, I closed the book, put it back, and rolled over. "Ugh... I should *not* be this tired on a weekend."

Making new friends, hanging out, trying my best to make it work. Was it...hurting me? No, not quite. It was just *exhausting*. I was being worn down, bit by bit. I mean, I was twisting myself into knots trying to avoid stepping on any toes, so of course I ended up overexerting myself.

Sometimes I contemplated whether it'd be easier to give up and ghost them entirely. In fact, I actually gave it a try one time—and that was when I met Adachi. Was that a good thing? I would've said yes.

The thing about being alone is that it's *boring*—an affliction far harder to cure than any simple loneliness. The only treatment for its debilitating malignancy is human connection. That was why I subjected myself to this steady erosion. I needed to wear myself down if I wanted to keep myself going.

Under my breath, I recited a line from the manga aloud, as if savoring every word.

"Don't blame me if it doesn't work out. I wasn't trying to hurt anyone."

5. Girls' Day Out

I WAS LYING IN BED after work on a weekday when my phone suddenly started ringing. It was Shimamura.

"Would you rather do karaoke, go to a restaurant, or go to the river?"

It was the first thing she said to me during our first-ever phone call. What kind of question was this? Was she trying to ask me on a date? No, probably not.

"Where did that come from?" I asked.

"Karaoke was my idea, Nagafuji suggested the restaurant, and Hino suggested the river."

So, this *was* some kind of outing. Evidently my guess wasn't far off...except that I didn't expect other people to be involved.

"Hino asked me to hang out this Sunday, and I figured I'd invite you."

"Oh. Gotcha. I don't know... I feel like it'd just be awkward if I went."

"Whoa... I didn't realize you cared about that stuff," Shimamura gasped, feigning shock.

Oh, come on. I laughed slightly. "What kind of jerk do you take me for?"

"A big—uh—proponent of not sweating the small stuff, that's all."

Were you about to call me "a big jerk"? Because that's a pretty jerk move, too. "I'm really not. Believe it or not, I care a lot about what other people think." *Especially you.* But I couldn't bring myself to say that part.

"Hmm." She didn't sound convinced. "Well, I'll just assume you're coming."

I hesitated for a moment, but ultimately gave in. "Uh...sure, why not."

After all, I hardly ever got the opportunity to hang out with her on a weekend. If I turned her down, I'd just end up spending the whole day in my room while she went off and had fun without me.

"So, where would you like to go? You can suggest somewhere else if you want."

"Wait, so...I'm the one who gets to decide where we're all going?"

"Probably."

"But I wasn't even originally invited... Now I feel bad."

"I'm pretty sure Hino would've invited you herself if she could've. She just doesn't have your number." At that, a smile crept onto my lips. Somehow, the fact that only Shimamura knew my number made me feel...secure. But I wasn't brave enough to follow that feeling to its logical conclusion, so I ignored it.

"I don't know... What would we do at the river?"

"Probably go fishing, since that's what Hino likes."

"Fishing...hmm."

I tried to imagine it, but it didn't feel right. Would the four of us just stand in a row, ankle-deep in ice-cold river water, waiting for something to bite while direct sunlight beat down on us? (Not that November weather was all that hot, but still.)

Personally, my family had never taken me on any nature trips as a kid, so when it came to the wild outdoors, the whole concept seemed joyless and tiring.

The restaurant option would probably see us spending a few hours at a Denny's or a McDonald's, eating and chatting. Would I be able to fit in? I couldn't think of any common ground between the four of us, which meant there wouldn't be much for me to talk about. In fact, I could easily picture myself sitting there in tedious silence for hours on end.

"Let's do karaoke, then."

Using the process of elimination, that seemed like the safest choice. We wouldn't need to talk much, and if there was a lull in the conversation, we could just focus on whoever was singing. Plus, it was Shimamura's idea, and I wanted to support it, even if it was something she chose at random.

"Okay! I'll let them know."

Hearing her voice on the other end of the line grow distant, I realized she was probably about to hang up, so I hastily called out to her. "Hey, uh, Shimamura?"

"Hmm?"

Sure enough, her voice was quieter now, as though she'd already pulled her phone away from her face. I knew that if I hesitated for even a moment, she would end the call.

So, I summoned all my courage and blurted out, "Would you wanna sing something together?"

"Sure, but what? I don't actually know what kind of music you listen to."

It took everything I'd had to ask that question, and yet she made it sound like no big deal. *Wait*. Hadn't we talked about music before? Going back through my memories, it felt as though we definitely had. Most likely she'd simply forgotten.

"I'd say I have pretty normal taste."

"Okay then, what's a 'normal' song to you?"

"Uhhh...I'm sure whatever you like is fine," I replied, after trying and failing to think of a specific example. *Ugh, why am I like this?*

"I wouldn't be so sure... I like a lot of oldies and stuff."

"How old are we talking? 'Old' as in music from before we were born?"

"Stuff from the nineties. You know, like *Robinson* by Spitz?"

"Oh, okay. I could probably sing that."

In fact, I didn't know that *Robinson* was a nineties song at all. I heard it every now and then on the radio, and it really didn't sound that old. That said, I didn't have the lyrics memorized, so I would need to look them up.

"Once Hino decides on the details, I'll let you know."

"Okay."

If Shimamura had given Hino my number, then she wouldn't have needed to call me back. Thus, it was a good thing that she hadn't. To me, anyway.

"Anyway, see you Sunday!"

Getting a little ahead of ourselves, are we?

"Uh...you know we have school tomorrow, right?" I asked.

"Oh, right. Okay, see you tomorrow!"

At times like these, I never knew exactly when to end the call, so often the other person and I would sit in awkward silence for a while until one of us figured it out. Not Shimamura, though—she hung up straight away. In a way, that really demonstrated who she was as a person.

I set my phone down, sat up, and looked at the calendar hanging on the wall. It was the first week of November, and today was Wednesday. There was still quite a while to go until Sunday.

At that point, I was attending class every day—and eating lunch with Shimamura once every three days. Nothing else worth mentioning. At my part-time job, I'd started to pay more attention to the parking lot's contents, since I was terrified Shimamura's family would come back for dinner again. But, other than that, nothing had really changed.

For the record, the family hadn't returned since the first time, probably because Shimamura didn't want her mom asking me any invasive questions. You'd think adults would still remember what it was like to be a teenager, yet they always seemed to forget after enough years passed. Was that just another part of growing up?

I let out what felt like my umpteenth sigh. *At least my life is less boring now, I guess.*

While I appreciated Shimamura's invite, I wasn't crazy about the prospect of her other friends being there. I knew I was being unreasonable, but I was still really frustrated.

Knowing Shimamura, she'd only invited me because Hino told her to. Obviously she wouldn't say it to my face, though, because she wanted to be polite. I appreciated that, too.

But it didn't change the fact that I was an afterthought.

Later that night, in bed, I thought back to the day we'd first met.

When I arrived at the gym loft, Shimamura was already there—sitting cross-legged on the floor on top of some green netting, as I recall. This was back when we were still wearing our summer uniforms, and I remember seeing a faint tan line on her arm.

She turned and noticed me, and our eyes met. She still carried that telltale junior-high vibe, which meant she was probably a first-year like me.

I didn't know her name, but it quickly became apparent that she knew mine.

"Adachi, right?"

"Uh…yeah?"

"We're in the same class."

She waved at me. Naturally, I didn't recognize her at all.

The second semester had just started, and compared to October, the temperature was *sweltering*. At least when you were outside, there was some small chance of a breeze, but in the loft? It felt like walking into an oven. As such, it didn't strike me as an ideal hideout in the least, especially since someone else had beaten me to it.

But I couldn't exactly respond to her enthusiastic "Hey, I know you!" with "Cool story, bye." We were in the same boat—both cutting class. And I was a tiny bit curious about what her reasons were.

With nowhere better to go, I sat down on the edge of a dusty old ping-pong table. When she introduced herself, she joked, "They call me Shimamura Co.," and just like that, I couldn't unsee it. Whenever I thought about her, I envisioned the store logo.

"You come here often?"

"Nah. Just felt like it today." I had been on my way to my usual spot when I noticed a teacher out on patrol, so I snuck into the loft to hide. Luckily, none of the classes were using the gym at the moment. "What about you?"

"Likewise."

I'd later learn that this was the first day Shimamura ever skipped class. She explained to me that she "couldn't get in the right headspace" for class after being away from school for so long, but I had no way of knowing if that was the truth. Maybe she was running from something. Maybe something had happened over summer break. But I didn't care as much back then, so I just let it go.

I sat a reasonable distance from Shimamura. The conversation had died, and all that flowed between us was our own sweat. She dabbed hers with a handkerchief; I took out a hand towel and wiped off whatever remained of my makeup.

In my boredom, I played around on my cell phone for a minute, but there wasn't much to do except check the time. *Ugh, why is lunch so far away?* I glanced at Shimamura and saw her staring blankly up at the window. At the time, I wondered what she was thinking about. Later, I'd learn that the answer was "nothing much."

Alone, the silence was tolerable. With someone else present, however, I was obliged to worry about whether silence made them uncomfortable, and I found that emotional labor needlessly exhausting.

Right around the time I started contemplating whether I should make an excuse to leave, however, I heard a loud chirping sound. Startled, I looked up...and realized a cicada clung to the window outside.

It was screaming with so much energy, you'd think this was still the height of August. Shimamura and I exchanged a glance, almost reflexively. We smiled awkwardly.

"So obnoxious."

"Totally."

She pushed herself to her feet, walked over to the window, and tapped on the glass. The cicada fell, possibly knocked loose by the vibration—I saw it try to flap its wings, and yet it plummeted straight down regardless. Shimamura hastily retracted her hand, then turned to look at me with an expression that said, "Oh crap."

At the time, I hoped desperately that she wasn't about to drag me into something. Sadly, I would *not* prove fortunate.

The cicada had fallen silent. For a while, Shimamura just stared out the window. Then, eventually, she turned and pointed to the stairs with the same finger that had just sent an annoying bug to its doom.

"Wanna go check on him?" she asked.

Evidently, she felt guilty for inadvertently causing the cicada's demise.

"Sure," I agreed, since I didn't have anything better to do. Maybe, once we were outside, I would find an excuse to part ways.

We headed down the stairs and walked out to the athletic field, where a group of male students unenthusiastically ran laps. Taking care to stay out of sight, we snuck around to the back of the building. There, growing all by itself in the shaded space between the gym and the martial-arts dojo, a single tall tree reached up to the loft window. At the base of its trunk was the cicada from earlier.

It lay on its back, frantically flapping its wings, but to no avail. Evidently this little bug was on its last legs and lacked the strength to right itself. I heard more cicadas above us in the tree, but they didn't seem to care that their friend had fallen. As a truant student, I found that I could relate.

Shimamura crouched down and reached out.

"Ew, you're gonna touch it?"

"These aren't that gross. But if it was a worm or a roly-poly, no way."

I didn't understand her benchmark for what made a cicada any less gross. Was it because they could fly? After a moment of contemplation, I decided that made sense. After all, I could see myself touching a ladybug, but not a centipede.

Shimamura picked up the cicada hesitantly. Naturally, it started squirming like crazy.

"Gah!"

She squirmed in kind, trying to put some distance between herself and the bug, but because she was *holding* it, that was obviously kind of impossible. *Don't you dare bring that thing over here.*

Eventually the two of them wore each other out, and they both calmed down. Shimamura paused, shook her head, and approached the tree.

"Climb on, little guy!"

She held the cicada to the tree trunk, and its legs began to flail again. But, when she let go, the bug had firmly attached itself to the bark and was screaming away once more. With our mission accomplished, we returned to the gym.

At some point I'd forgotten to make an excuse to slip away, but oh well. I didn't feel like it anymore.

As we climbed the loft stairs, Shimamura asked me, "How many more days do you think he'll live for?"

"No clue," I answered honestly.

"Yeah, me neither," she replied.

There was a brief pause as we arrived at the landing. Then I asked her, "How long would you *want* it to live?"

She stopped to consider this. "I'll say...fifteen more days."

Sure enough, fifteen days later, she came to the loft with dirt on her palms. If I had to guess, she was probably out digging a grave for the cicada.

That was the story of how Shimamura and I first met...
back when I didn't yet consider her a friend.

As was typically the case whenever I met up with
Shimamura, I was nervous for a variety of reasons.

On my bike, I passed through a shopping district
(mostly dead, save for a confectionery store and a bike repair shop), crossed over the long-disused railroad tracks,
and made a left. There, I spotted our meetup location
just ahead.

Sure enough, once I passed the bank and the bus stop,
I noticed Shimamura leaning against the post office sign
out front. Come to think of it, she was oddly diligent
about these things. Why else was she always the first to
arrive whenever we met up?

She waved at me, and I waved back shyly as I rolled
toward her.

"You know, for a girl who's always late to class, you
sure are punctual when it comes to hanging out!"

"Pot, meet kettle," I replied.

Personally, I was just relieved to see that the sparkly
girl wasn't with her this time. I wouldn't put it past
Shimamura to randomly encounter her in the street and

bring her along "for fun." Who *was* she, anyway? I knew Shimamura was probably just being nice and humoring her, but…I mean, the hair? The eyes? Clearly, she had to come from another planet, right?

"Cool clothes—where'd you get them? Shimamura Co.?"

"Gee, I've never heard that one before," Shimamura replied, pinching the hem of her white knitted sweater with a scowl.

Instantly I regretted what I'd said. Apparently, her other friends had already made that joke, and I did *not* want to be like them.

"I'm surprised you didn't wear your Chinese dress."

"Oh, shut up."

Shimamura didn't have a bike with her; evidently, she'd walked here. As we waited for the others, she wandered in circles around the parking lot, and I watched her from a distance. I was tempted to strike up a conversation…but I couldn't think of a topic.

I never used to pay so much attention to Shimamura before, but now I hyper-fixated on her every move. Lately I noticed her appearance a lot more often, too. She was just *really* pretty.

"Hey, so…"

"Hmm?" She turned in my direction as she walked around and around in a figure-eight shape.

"I memorized those lyrics."

"Huh? What lyrics...? Oh, right! For our duet."

For a second there, I was scared she'd forgotten, so those last few words came as an immense relief.

"If we have any other songs in common, we should sing those, too."

"Yeah."

There was still no sign of the other two girls...and I was tempted to steal Shimamura and go somewhere else. But just then, almost as if karma read my mind, I spotted Hino and Nagafuji on the bridge to our right, riding tandem on a bicycle. The short one did the pedaling, and the tall one sat there idly with her hands resting on the other girl's shoulders. It looked so backward, I couldn't help but laugh.

"Oh, hey, they're here!"

Shimamura stepped out into the street to flag them down, and they each responded by waving both hands. *Wait, don't do that! That's dangerous!*

With no grip on the handlebars, the girls rolled down the bridge's slope and coasted right over to us, using the soles of their shoes to brake. *Weirdos.* Hino grinned at me like she could hear what I was thinking.

Meanwhile, Nagafuji leapt off the bike.

"You still don't know how to ride a bike?" Shimamura asked her.

"Of course not," she replied coolly, and it was then that I realized she wasn't wearing her glasses today. As a result, her almond-shaped eyes were more pronounced. Oddly enough, the lack of glasses actually *increased* her usual "intellectual" vibe, something I didn't know was possible. *Isn't it usually the other way around?*

Nagafuji and Hino approached me.

"Hey there, Ada-chee!" Hino greeted me casually. That was actually the same nickname I'd had in grade school. Truth be told, I didn't really see the point in a "nickname" that sounded identical to my actual last name.

"Hiya, Ada-chee!" Nagafuji repeated playfully.

"Ada-chee!" Shimamura chimed in with a grin. Reflexively I looked away, fighting the impulse to pull my cardigan hood over my face.

Hino and Nagafuji aside, I was viscerally opposed to Shimamura calling me that for some reason. Well...okay, not "opposed," per se. Just...self-conscious...? In other words, I was embarrassed. To distract myself, I turned and straddled my bike.

"Which way to the karaoke place?" I asked, hoping a little bike ride would cool my burning cheeks.

"That way," said Hino, pointing in the direction from which I'd come, toward a building just across the street.

The sign out front, which read something-I-couldn't-make-out Village, advertised "BBQ, BUFFET, KARAOKE, AND CHILDCARE." That struck me as an incongruent mess, and yet the parking lot was packed full of cars.

Also...if the building was ten seconds away on foot, then why did we bother meeting up at the post office at all? With a sigh, I hopped off my bike and decided to push it along instead. *Ugh, I look like a loser.*

"I'm surprised you actually showed up," Hino mused.

"I know, right?" Shimamura agreed.

Both of them were looking at me, so I knew they were talking about me. But what I didn't understand was why they seemed to want me to explain why I'd showed up. If I told them my real reason for coming, they'd think I was a total creep. I could only imagine the weird looks they'd give me.

"I didn't have anything better to do," I lied. Thinking about it, that was probably the reason why people saw me as aloof and bitchy. Admittedly, I *did* have trouble fitting into social situations... Maybe I just hadn't had enough experience, in which case today would serve as good practice for me.

"Aha. 'Because I was bored'—the ultimate motivation for any Shinigami. Excellent." Hino nodded to herself. Was she referencing something? I didn't get it.

The karaoke parlor's interior was dimly lit, decorated with pumpkins and metallic black curtains. Halloween had been weeks ago, but apparently this place didn't get the memo. On the right was a sofa set, where two elderly men sat playing a leisurely game of Othello. In fact, there were groups of old people everywhere I looked, and by contrast, the four of us stuck out like a sore thumb. The old people didn't seem suspicious of us, probably because we were just kids in their eyes, but I didn't enjoy getting stared at, regardless of the reason.

On the wall was a sign with the price breakdown. Weekends cost 180 yen per thirty minutes, or 360 yen for an hour. That was a lot cheaper than the karaoke place at the station square. The sign also advertised something called the "Nine-Hour Special," but I couldn't say I was interested. If we spent nine hours here, we wouldn't leave until really late, and I had work tonight.

"Should we do four hours to start?" Hino asked us. To me, that still seemed like an excessive amount of time.

"That makes sense," Nagafuji replied.

Does it? I guess it does.

As for Shimamura, she stayed silent, toying with a strand of her hair.

Hino went ahead and paid for four hours. As it turned

242

out, the employees were all elderly, too. *Why did she bring us here, of all places? I guess that's Hino for you.*

Next, she led us to a room at the end of the hall. Maybe this part was no big deal for everyone else, but for me, it was nerve-wracking. Having to decide where to sit always stressed me out.

The room was fairly cramped, with white walls and two black sofas. I saw Shimamura head for the sofa on the right-hand side, so I casually followed. My legs felt a little stiff and robotic, but in the end, I succeeded in sitting next to her. Hino and Nagafuji sat down on the opposite sofa.

Maybe this seating arrangement would've happened regardless, but for me, it was *essential*.

"Can I put our bags here?" asked Shimamura.

"Sure," I nodded, biting back a grin as I triumphantly reveled in my accomplishment. It wasn't like I'd need my phone for anything, much less any of the other stuff in my bag. Plus, my bike key was safely in my pocket.

I reached for the menu on the table. I wasn't especially hungry, but I wanted something to look at while I waited. Unfortunately, Nagafuji grabbed it a split-second ahead of me. I shrank back; she gave me a look that said, "You sure you don't want it?" I held up a hand in a "no, you keep it" gesture.

Meanwhile, Hino struck a dramatic pose as she turned the mic on. "All right, I'll go first! *The vortex of tiiiime—*"

"Stop that." Nagafuji promptly confiscated the mic from Hino, which I appreciated. Why sing without actually inputting the song into the system?

"Okay, fine! I'll sing something else," Hino conceded, and the mic was swiftly returned. "Uhhhh..."

She punched her song of choice into the remote—a children's song, for some reason. As she sang, she peered down at the menu lying open in Nagafuji's lap. Then she pointed at an item.

"If we're getting a pitcher, get green tea—it's better for your throat, compared to oolong. At least, that's what my favorite teacher told me."

"Who are you talking about?" asked Shimamura.

"Mr. S, the karaoke lover."

"That still sounds like you're dodging the question." Annoyed, Shimamura scowled. Our homeroom teacher's last name started with a T, so it had to be someone else.

After Hino finished her children's song, she held the mic up. "Who's next?"

Out of the corner of my eye, I glanced at Shimamura, who was reading the leaflets on the table. Before long, she sensed my gaze and looked up. Our eyes met, and then she gave me a look that asked, "Wanna sing together?"

I hastily shook my head. *Not yet.*

"Okay, my turn!" Nagafuji announced as she took the mic.

Hino put a hand on her hip. "Do you even know the words to any songs?"

"Uhhhh...ummmm..." Nagafuji hesitated. Somehow she still looked dignified, even when she stared at the floor. "I'll just have you sing all the parts I don't know!"

"So, you want me to sing *another* song by myself? It's turning into a one-woman show over here!"

Despite that statement's implication, Nagafuji didn't seem offended in the least. Apparently she had some sort of memory problem; she couldn't even remember my name unless someone reminded her. She opened the song book and started to hunt through it for a song number, and it occurred to me that Hino must have put a number in completely at random.

A short while later, our pitcher of green tea arrived, delivered to us by—you guessed it—another elderly man. Absently, I wondered exactly how old all the staff were. We poured four cups of tea, and after we shared a formal toast, Nagafuji added her song to the system: a slightly older tune by an artist named Nijou Owari.

The song itself was too upbeat for my taste, but I liked the piano accompaniment, as well as the person playing it, who was known for only ever wearing kimonos. I once read an interview she'd done in a magazine; she and the singer spent the whole thing talking about some dog. And, when someone asked her about music, she started talking about a diner she went to.

"Do you know this one?" Shimamura asked me between sips of tea.

I nodded. "I don't know the lyrics, but yeah."

"Huh. I've never heard it before," she replied, seemingly uninterested, and took another sip.

She was really going hard on the tea—not because she was actually thirsty, but purely out of restless anxiety. That much was obvious, even to an outside observer like me. Try as she might to act as though she was right at home in this environment, I could tell she was forcing it—especially compared to her usual behavior in the gym loft. Like it or not, this was outside her comfort zone.

Perhaps she and I actually approached social situations with a similar mindset, but she was simply better at hiding it. Maybe that was why I found myself drawn to her—because we were birds of a feather. Whenever we were in a group of four, it became painfully apparent how much better-off Shimamura and I were when it was just the two of us.

In the end, Hino ended up taking over most of the second song, too. Afterward, she held the mic in our direction. "Your turn!" she grinned.

Shimamura and I exchanged a glance...and what followed was the world's shortest game of hot potato.

"If we're going clockwise, then it's *your* turn."

"Hmmm...okay, I know what we're doing." Shimamura took the mic. "Could you get us another one?" she asked Hino. Then she grabbed me by the arm and pulled me to my feet. "We're doing a duet!"

As we scooted around the table to the front of the room, I hesitated. This was happening way too soon. Still, I could tell Shimamura wasn't serious about forcing me into it—just guiding me along.

She grabbed the remote and punched in the number. Apparently, she'd looked it up in advance. My heart thumped in my chest, begging her to slow down. It felt as though a hand pressed my back, pushing me forward against my will.

I was never great at singing in front of an audience, and I always hated graded performances in music class. But today I would be singing with Shimamura. Simple stage fright was the *least* of my worries now.

We stood side by side, almost like we were standing at a teacher's podium to give a class presentation. I was so nervous, my stomach was in knots...and, as the opening notes played, I started to feel lightheaded. But right as I began to worry that I was going to pass out, Shimamura spoke suddenly.

"I actually really appreciate you coming up to sing with me."

"Huh?" Where had *that* come from?

Smiling, she switched on her mic. "I'm not great at singing in front of people, you know?"

"Don't make excuses, you wet blanket! Just do it!" Hino jeered playfully from her seat. Meanwhile, Nagafuji was busy ordering something else off the menu.

As for me, well... Shimamura's little confession brought a smile to my face. *She's the same way!* My heart fluttered with joy. It felt as though we'd grown that much closer.

"Same, actually. I'm glad you're up here with me," I told her.

Then the prelude ended, and it was time to sing...so I poured my heart into it.

Once our allotted four hours were up, we wound up getting an extension. In the end, we left after five hours of singing. The others made me get up and sing by myself several times, and I had to fight the urge to crawl in a hole and die...but Shimamura told me I did great, so maybe it was all worth it.

Now I was starting to understand exactly what it was I wanted from her.

By the time we left the karaoke parlor, it was already three o'clock. The sun was out, but the temperature was notably milder compared to the previous month's weather. Winter was on the way, and soon this year would come to an end. Functionally speaking, however, January wasn't *that* much different from December. The numbers on the calendar would change, but that was about it.

"Did you have a good time, my dear Ada-chee?" asked Hino.

I wish she wouldn't go out of her way to ask me my opinion—it makes me feel like an outsider. Which I am, technically, but still. And I notice she's still calling me Ada-chee.

"Yeah, it was fun," I replied, glancing at Shimamura out of the corner of my eye. She looked back at me with a patronizing smile, as if to say "Good for you!" It was almost like she was my mom or something.

If anyone else tried to act like that, I would've ripped them a new one...but, because it was her, I was fine with it. Happy, even.

"Glad to hear it! We'll be sure to invite you again sometime. And by 'we,' I mean Shimamura."

"Why me? I mean...not that I mind." For a split-second, she made a face like, "Why don't *you* do it?" Classic Shimamura.

Then Hino patted me on the shoulder and hopped onto her bike, a knowing grin on her face. "Welp, see you folks tomorrow!"

What had *that* been about?

Hino waved at us; I waved back slightly. Then Nagafuji walked up to her. "Are you sure you know where I live?"

"Do you think I'm stupid or something? Remind me again who picked your ass up this morning?"

Bickering, they sped off down the street toward the bridge. They were nothing if not close friends, but I didn't appreciate their overly familiar attitude toward me. I'd intentionally kept a respectable distance from them, but nevertheless, they were starting to treat me like their little buddy.

Not that I hated them, per se... I just wasn't used to that sort of personality. None of my other friends were ever quite that forward with me.

"Well, now that I'm done entertaining *them*, I guess it's time to go home and entertain my sister!" Shimamura joked with a giggle. With that, our fun little moment finished; she turned and started walking. To me, it felt like she was hanging up on me all over again. She was always so quick to end things—I wished she would give me enough time to properly articulate my thoughts. Instead, I blurted them out.

"Want me to...take you home?"

She stopped short. My hand slipped off the brake, and I slid a bit too far forward.

"It's not that far from here, right? And, uh...I wouldn't want you to have to walk all that way."

Belatedly I realized the contradiction in what I had just said. Shimamura looked confused, too. Maybe I shouldn't have tried to come up with an excuse.

She glanced over at Hino and Nagafuji's figures steadily retreating into the distance, then donned a smile. "Sure, I'll catch a ride with you."

What a relief.

She placed her bookbag into my bike basket, put her hand on my shoulder, and hopped on.

"Take me away, Ada-chee!"

"Okay, no. *You* have to call me by my actual name," I insisted, glancing at her over my shoulder.

She looked at me in surprise, her eyes wide. "It's not that drastically different, is it? Do you not like nicknames or something? And why am I the only one not allowed?"

"It's not that. I don't have anything against you in particular..." *But if you wanted to come up with your own unique nickname for me, I'd be okay with that.*

Instead of finishing my thought, however, I started pedaling—slowly at first, as I struggled with the added weight, then gradually faster and faster over time. Although I enjoyed the thrill of the escalating speed, I didn't want to get there *too* quickly, so I kept my pace in check.

The mere thought of going to Shimamura's house made me dizzy. No way could I go back in there today— maybe not ever. I was still traumatized from last time.

"Make a right here, then go straight for a while."

"Okay."

I took a right turn, as requested. We sailed down the footpath that crossed the abandoned railroad tracks, then headed through the shopping district on a path so narrow, I could only hope we wouldn't encounter anyone else headed in our direction.

"For real, though, did you have fun?" Shimamura asked me after a few minutes.

"Kinda," I replied honestly, since it was just the two of us. I didn't exactly have the time of my life, and if Shimamura hadn't been there, I would've found an excuse to leave early.

After spending the day in a group setting, I was once again viscerally reminded that my feelings for Shimamura were different.

I didn't mind the prospect of being friends with Hino and Nagafuji—but *only* friends. I was fine hanging out with them over the weekend, but not on a special holiday like Christmas. That was how I knew I only thought of them as friends.

Shimamura, though? I *did* want to spend Christmas with her. And not just Christmas, either—New Year's, and Valentine's Day, and all the holidays after that. I wanted to be close to her...and now, I was starting to understand why.

Most likely, what I wanted from Shimamura was the familial affection of a sister or a mom. It was hard to put into words, but basically, I wanted someone to hold me... to protect me...to *accept* me. Probably because my relationship with my real family left a lot to be desired.

If I ever admitted that, though, I knew I'd sound like a total child. And I'd sooner have died than told Shimamura that I wanted her to be my oneechan.

"Oh, actually, could you make a left here?" she asked suddenly.

Intrigued, I did as she requested. Up ahead, I spotted a deserted plot of land, covered in a fine layer of sand and dotted with children's play equipment—a park, in other words. Back in preschool, I used to *love* playing around on the jungle gym.

"Wow. Your house looks really different from the last time I visited," I joked.

"I know, right? Who needs walls or indoor plumbing? Ha ha ha. Anyway, shut up and pull over, would you?"

I slowed to a stop next to the playground. Shimamura hopped off and headed across the sandy ground to the vending machine nearby. As I locked up my bike, she called out to me, "I was thirsty, so I wanted to stop for a drink real quick. What kind would you like? My treat!"

Something about her offer reminded me of our lunch conversations back when we used to cut class.

"Do they have mineral water?"

"Nope, just canned drinks. Is Pocari Sweat okay?"

"Uhhhh...sure."

She returned carrying two cans, and together we walked through the playground. There were plenty of benches to sit on, but instead we headed for the swing set, where we each took a seat. Her swing was yellow and mine was red, though the paint was peeling; when I touched the chains, rust residue got all over my fingers. When I wiped it away, it crumbled into nothing, just like old memories. But only the good ones; the bad memories liked to stick around.

"Thanks for hanging in there," she said as she handed me my drink.

"Oh, please," I laughed, shaking my head. "We were just hanging out."

"But it's still out of your comfort zone, right?"

"Well... Maybe..."

"If you don't want me to invite you anymore, I'll stop."

There she goes, treating me like a little kid. I shook my head slightly. After all, if Shimamura was the person inviting me, then that meant she'd be going, too. "That's okay. I really don't mind it, so feel free to keep inviting me."

"You sure?" she replied, then sipped her drink. A moment later, she started to sway back and forth on her swing, and I sensed that she was bored. I stared down at my can of Pocari, then took a tiny sip.

For a Sunday afternoon, this place was *really* deserted. Here I was, alone with Shimamura...but I couldn't afford to let my guard down. Somehow it felt like that glitter-girl was going to pop out right when I least expected it, like a ghost. A sparkly blue ghost.

"So, what's up?" Shimamura asked out of the blue, peering at me as the swings creaked under our weight. I didn't know what she was talking about, so I gave her a funny look. "Oh... Well..." She paused for a moment. "You were looking at me an awful lot during karaoke, so I thought maybe there was something you wanted to talk about."

I nearly jumped out of my skin. She was on to me. Admittedly, yes, we had made eye contact numerous times in the karaoke room, but I didn't realize she noticed me looking all the other times, too. My spike in tension radiated through my body to the swing, and the chains rattled in response—a reflection of my own internal panic.

I averted my eyes. The blood rushed to my head as I contemplated how to respond. *For starters, I'll play dumb and see where that gets me.*

"Was I?"

"Yeah," she nodded. I shrank down slightly, but continued to feign innocence.

"Are you sure you're not just paranoid?"

"I literally *saw* you looking at me. Multiple times."

Indeed she had. Each time she caught me, I'd tried to play it off by smiling vaguely, but apparently that didn't work. I glanced at her out of the corner of my eye, hoping to gauge her reaction.

"There! You just did it again!"

Guilty as charged. I hastily averted my gaze.

Did I actually want to talk to her about something? Plenty of things, sure. But I knew that the second I tried, she'd get weirded out and run away, so I hesitated. Faltered. Festered.

My feelings built and built inside my chest, blossoming, ripening—but fragile. After enough time, they would rot on the vine and fall forgotten to the ground. A tiny sapling had sprouted up from my heart to my mouth, climbing like ivy in search of the sun. I tried to hold it back, but couldn't stop myself in time.

My breathing grew so labored, I sounded like a panting dog. I lowered my head in Shimamura's direction.

"Could you...pet me?"

All I could say to myself in response to that was... *Wow*. I understood *why* I'd said it, but that didn't make it any less cringeworthy. I was terrified to see the look on her face. I got the feeling I would plummet face-first into the sand if I let go of my swing.

"Hmm."

Her response was curt and detached, like a scientist observing her lab rat. Meanwhile, I could feel her looking at my head. I started to sweat. My throat trembled with the impulse to scream, "Just kidding!" The vibrations traveled to my arms. *I take it back. I take it back. I take it back.*

For a long, agonizing moment, I found myself torn between regret, despair, and something else entirely. Then—right as I gave in and looked up—I felt a tiny fingertip brush my bowed head, light as a feather.

"Whoa," I murmured reflexively. My heart lit up like fireworks.

At first, she tapped me lightly on the scalp as though testing the water. Then her small, dainty hand cupped my head and slowly stroked my hair. Were her fingers running through my hair, or was my hair running through her fingers? After a while, I couldn't tell.

"You're such a needy baby."

I seemed to remember her making a similar comment at some point in the past. As with the last time, I was too shy to look at her, so I couldn't see her expression. Was she exasperated with me, or merely amused? There was no loud gust of wind to interrupt us—almost as though the planet itself was frozen in time, just for this single moment.

My heart pounded like crazy, but my mind was mournfully calm—a striking contrast that made it clear to me just how separate those things were. I could tell that my head was leaning into her palm, silently imploring her to continue.

"More?"

Her palm brushed over my bangs. I nodded wordlessly, and she ran her hand gently over my head. Every time her fingers slid through my hair, my mind went blank. If I'd had a tail, I would've been wagging it like crazy right about now.

Clearly, something was deeply wrong with me. Was I stupid, or merely some kind of freak? Probably both. Maybe I'd be better off wondering what the stupid-to-freak ratio looked like.

"Is that enough?"

I felt myself wanting to ask for more, so I pursed my lips and nodded instead. "Mm-hmm."

She pulled her hand away, and I summoned all the courage I could find to raise my head and look at her. She was smiling and rubbing her fingers together.

"You'd better not start calling me Oneechan at school," she warned jokingly.

"No promises," I replied with a self-deprecating laugh.

She must have felt as awkward as I did, because she started to chug her drink. Once the can was empty, she held out her free hand in my direction. "Here, I'll go throw them away."

"Oh, uh...I'm not done with mine. I'm gonna take it home and finish it later."

"Oh, okay."

She got up and walked to the trash to dispose of her can. Once I'd made sure she wasn't watching, I tilted my can upside-down. Bone dry. I was a liar.

Truthfully, I planned to take it home and decorate my room with it. Was that creepy? Maybe so. But I knew

Shimamura would never see my room... So, if it didn't hurt anyone, and it made me happy, then where was the harm? *One girl's trash is another girl's treasure.*

My scalp continued to tingle long after the head pats stopped. I got up and carefully set my empty can into my bike basket. Then Shimamura returned, and we got ready to take off.

Once I'd unlocked the bicycle chain and straddled the seat, she climbed on behind me. The feeling of her hand on my shoulder made me nervous. I thought back to the time I'd held that hand in mine, and my cheeks flushed. I started to pedal, keeping my head tilted down. After all, sunset was still a few hours away, so I couldn't blame any redness on a mere trick of the light.

Together on my bicycle, Shimamura and I left the park. Ten minutes from now, as with all good things, this private moment we'd shared would come to an end.

But hey, that rarity is part of what makes it so special, right? It's fun to go diving, but eventually you have to come up for air. Then, once you've caught your breath, you can go back under and keep searching for more buried treasure.

I wanted my relationship with Shimamura to be special. Not necessarily in a weird way—no, really. But then again, I wasn't opposed to that, either...which meant that I was probably in love with her.

Afterword

DON'T WORRY—nobody dies in this one.

Anyway, hello. My editor asked me to "write something like *Yuru Yuri*," so here it is. Looking back, I think the title I referenced was one letter off...

Nothing else to write!

"I saw a zashiki-warashi! Walked right past my bedroom door in the middle of the night! It wore a red kimono and everything!"

No, Dad—that was me.

To my poor, delusional father, my *[redacted]* mother, and all the readers out there, no matter how you came across this book: thank you so much.

—Hitoma Iruma